WINDOWS TO THE SOUL

P. FLORES

WINDOWS TO THE SOUL

Publisher: BoD – Books on Demand, Stockholm, Sweden
Printer: BoD – Books on Demand, Norderstedt, Germany
ISBN: 978-91-7969-969-7

INDEX

CHAPTER 1:
THE PLAN

So…what time shall I pick you up?" he said, cheeks red like a tomato. You could tell he didn't do this very often, but neither did she. She was calm, on the outside but inside she knew that the only reason was to be left alone once and for all.

"Um…how about 6 pm, after work, we could just go for a burger and just you know, talk. I barely know you and it would be nice to you know, at least pretend to be mad about each other."

"Yeah, you're right. I'm sorry, it's just that it feels odd you know. You don't want to date me and still be willing to sacrifice time for this." He said a bit uncertain, like it was an insult.

"It's not that, you're a nice guy and in other circumstances, I would be thrilled but this now it's not for the best. I'm not there, I'm only doing this to be left alone. My colleagues won't leave me unless I find someone and you're the only one who can save me. I'm sorry, we'll make a great day out of this and then, everything will be alright." She said, putting her hand on his arm.

She normally avoided touching anyone but this time, he needed comforting. He smiled, placed his hand on hers and pat it gently. "I'm in, I'll be happy to help you. So… what will we do when they're you know, in the office?"

"Hugs in the beginning, I'm totally okay with that. Kisses, well…on the cheek is also okay. In a month or so, we can kiss you know but no tongue…I've never done that and frankly I just don't think it's a good idea.

In 6 months, we can tell them it didn't work out and part ways as friends. That's the plan, what do you think?" she said and felt a bit restless.

She hadn't kissed a guy since high school and that was barely a kiss, she did love him though. Thomas was a big part of her life, and he was the first guy she kissed on the lips, they were after all dating. Well, at least so she thought after staying loyal to him for 1 ½ years to find out he was cheating 6 months back with one of her friends. Since that moment, she only kissed one other guy: Manuel from camp. He on the other hand didn't cheat, he wasn't ashamed of her and he did like her. In fact, they never broke up…

Anyhow, now everything was working towards the perfect fake relationship without dying in the process. Luckily, David was one of those guys that could help in any situation, even though they only knew each other a few months. He wasn't bad, kind of cute even but she just wasn't interested. All her life Celia had been alone, apart from those 2 guys in her life. Then of course was John, her biggest regret since they were remarkably close and could've become more in the end of high school. He saved her more than once in the hallway from nosy classmates, but after the graduation they lost contact and about 2 years later he moved into her building with his wife.

She was happy about him though, since they stayed friends until they never saw each other again. Celia kept studying and began working later, where she met regret number 2: a doctor named Tom. He was the sweetest guy and pretty much in love with her, but she was too shy to take another step closer.

They had a lot of close encounters like lunch times or afternoon snacks but more than that, nothing.

Once she managed to ask him if he had a girlfriend to which he replied: "No, I just date my sofa". But before she could ask him more, he was moved to another department and that was it. They did run into each other years later, said hi and still as shy as ever, she didn't ask him anything more.

Celia moved on, away from guys. She fell for some, but from a distance everything looked better, she couldn't manage to take more steps into having a relationship because she was afraid. Afraid that it would happen again, to be cheated on, to be lost in someone that she barely could recognize herself… No, no it would not come to that. She was strong enough to stay away from guys, in hope that when the right one would come along there wouldn't be any doubts. When the right man would come along, he would love her just as she was. No changes, no surgeries, no fake…just her.

But she knew that it was lie. Men lie, it's kind of their nature. Well women lie too, maybe not for the same reasons though. At least not her.

Today was a new day, Celia was walking in the sunshine on her way to work. Funny enough that it didn't feel grim to get up in the morning. Maybe because she had a plan, to finally make them understand that she didn't need a man in her life. She could do so much by herself: she had travelled within Europe and Latin America; her next plan was to visit the US and Hawaii.

All that she did by herself, afraid yes but it didn't feel scary at all. God was with her.

"Hey, there she is…someone left this for you." Andy said smiling, she recognized the scheming smile. A bouquet of flowers, red and pink roses with a small card closed in an envelope. Wow, David really did an effort to make this believable.

"To Celia, light of my life. With love, David" Oh jeez, this man is giving it away to quickly!! She smiled, pretending it was a surprise. "Aww he's sweet."

"Well, what did he say?" said Andy trying to read the card. "That's private! But he likes me, and I think I like him too." She said and put the card in her bag. The flowers were in water, but she put them on the common table in front of the lounge sofa.

She put on the computer and opened all the portals she used daily, a message popped up: From David: "Hi, sorry for the flowers. These aren't part of the plan, I just wanted to give you something to remember me by. Hope you like. D."

Oh God, what was he doing? She just agreed to keep it casual until some months pass but he's really pushing it. She wrote an email back:

"Hi, saw them and thank you. They're lovely and it's overly sweet but aren't you going from zero to 100 now? We haven't even had a date yet. Maybe we should talk about that. Call me during lunch. Take care/C."

That was a cold message, she thought to herself. Maybe I should try to be more, female-ish. Celia wasn't used to be the girlie girl, more like Lara Croft, apart from the knives and cool ass kicking vibe. She picked up the phone and dialed David's number, answering machine:

"Hi David, it's me. Sorry for the cold email, I think I panicked. You know, I'm not used to have someone liking me or thinking of me more than just "office rat". Thank you, the flowers are beautiful, and I took a picture. I'm keeping the card, I have this dorky box of old keepsakes and this one is a keeper. Talk soon, bye."

She felt strange, almost unrecognizable. What was her biggest fear? That it might work? That she could have a relationship with this guy, marriage and maybe even a family? No, no. But why not? There was nothing wrong with her as a person, apart from her fear of relationships and men. That fear came from a trauma back in the day, that guy that ruined her life but also her father's abandonment. She grew up with her mother and grandparents, they were her parents, the ones that went to parent teacher night or picked her up from school.

Celia missed her family, especially grandpa, her father in so many ways. The one supposed to accompany her to the altar when she would have gotten married, died 3 years ago and it almost killed her not being able to say goodbye. Tears were running down her cheeks as she remembered his smile, the chocolate bar in his pocket or his way of teaching her about a skeletal anatomy. My grandpa, she thought and grabbed the small chain she wore around her neck, it was his.

"Hey, are you okay?" a voice said, she looked up and it was him. It was David.

"Yeah, yeah I'm fine. It's just, I was thinking about my grandpa and I, I…" she couldn't hold back anymore. He immediately came to her side of the desk and held her in his arms, his hands stroking her back. She moved a little and he looked into her brown, tearful eyes. Before she knew and could wipe her tears, he caressed one away before leaning in on a soft kiss on the lips. Celia was in shock, but her brain sent a signal to continue the kiss. Now she leaned in, and he met her halfway, it was almost like getting electrocuted. She couldn't move away but she didn't want to either, instead she stayed in his arms until he finished the kiss and smiled. "I, I don't know what to say. But I'm not sorry for this, not for a second Celia. I like you too much, I don't know what…" Before he could finish the sentence, she was kissing him again. This time it was different, it felt natural, almost like when she dreamt of dating a leading guy from a movie. David was here, he comforted her, he wanted to help her in getting rid of her nosy colleagues, but it was more than that.

Did she love him? No, no it wasn't that kind of love but affection yes, or I don't know, maybe she just felt lonely.
  "Wow, that was…that was…" he said, trying to catch some air and she couldn't stop smiling. "I know, I didn't mean to you know but I, I think this is something else." She said and let him go, she adjusted her dress and moved away. It was shameful to be like this, so attached, so needy.

CHAPTER 2:
THE KISS AFTERMATH

Celia, I like you. I do, trust me this was great! But I don't want to be just that, some help in your life to get rid of them. I want us to be more. Just, give me a chance." David said moving closer to her chair, she stared at the floor, partially ashamed for what she just did but also for those words…she wouldn't have let anyone to use her like that, why should she? He deserved better.

"David, I…I don't know what flew into me. But I don't want to hurt you. I don't know if I can make this work, I don't know how to be a girlfriend." Celia said without lifting her eyes towards David, whom by now stood again by her side, put his arms around her shoulders and pushed her closer to his stomach. She laughed a bit when she heard his stomach growl and he kneeled in front of her to hug her properly and took a deep breath to feel her perfume. Calvin Klein never smelled so good. "Well, I think we need something to eat. Maybe talk about us for a while, not as partners in crime but more partners. What do you fancy?"

Celia was scared but somehow it felt right, he felt right, she smiled and said "I'll be happy to have a good steak and fries, but for now…I just want to kiss you again."

Did she just say that? This strange feeling, she felt was warming and reassuring, all she knew was that she couldn't stay away from his lips any longer. David took her hands, kissed them, and embraced her. When both let go, they engaged in a kiss again. They moved towards an empty couch, and he laid backwards to have her by his side.

He stroked her back, while she smelled his aftershave, they stayed like that for a while. It was a warm afternoon with a slight breeze, they were all alone and just enjoyed the silence. "You know, there's this great steakhouse in the city. How about we go there for some food and then we can, go for a walk?" he said, kissing her head and continued to stroke her back.

"Mm…that sounds great. But this is cozy, to stay like this. I like your arms…to be like this with you." She said and looked up to his face, who beamed at the sight of her big brown eyes. "We can go to my place after dinner, my couch is big enough for both of us." He said, hoping that he didn't ruin the moment, Celia was after all extremely sensitive and easily frightened in these kinds of situations that she almost was like a deer.

Celia sat up carefully, David right behind her and wrapped his arms around her. She smiled, the fright was silently quieting down and maybe the relationship wasn't all bad. Maybe it wasn't her the problem lied but with the guys she was interested in.

"So…want to go for a ride?" David said and kissed her cheek, she turned around to respond "Car?" He smiled, showing off his keys "Yeah, it's parked in the garage. Shall we?"

Celia took his hand and he put his arm around her, her feeling of panic was rising again but the thought of not kissing him again ever made her hold him even tighter. In the parking lot he clicked the key to open the car, before he let her in, he embraced her again and leaned in for a kiss.

She couldn't resist him, responded until he whispered, "If I could choose something in my life, would be to stay like this forever." She smiled, it almost felt like she was a teenager again but only with a more mature man. "Me too David, I don't know why I was so afraid of dating you."

Dinner at the steakhouse was great. They talked, laughed, shared anecdotes of their lives before meeting, suddenly Celia's phone rang "Hi mom, yeah sorry. I'm having dinner with a friend, oh okay, yeah, I'll just finish up and go. Okay, okay, bye."

"Sorry, I have to go…my mom needed me to stop by and do some grocery shop on my way home. Can we continue this tomorrow?" she said and put her phone in her bag.

"Sure, sure. Want me to drive you to a supermarket?" David said and called the waiter for the check. Celia stood up and grabbed her bag, leaned towards him, kissing him a long time. "That would be nice, sure you don't mind?"

He was still recovering from their kiss and said "Not at all…besides, I think I need one more of those before letting you go. Come on!" David was a gentleman, he paid before grabbing her hand and we headed out towards the car. He opened the door and let her in, he couldn't believe that she was his girlfriend. But was she? He didn't ask her properly, just a bunch of kisses and no direct proposal. He should address this right away.

"So, um, which supermarket? There's one of those big ones like 15 minutes away or do you prefer something close to home?" he began, starting the car and headed out of the parking lot.

She smiled, it didn't matter to her. "Take the one you said, let's see if I can find some good bread, my sister is so picky!"

He smiled back, he didn't want to ruin their perfect evening. At some points he put his hand on hers and she squeezed it back, but he knew he had to ask. "Celia, um…I don't want this night to end but I need to ask you something. Is this real? I mean us, are we together now?"

She turned her head, not surprised nor worried but happy. In the stop sign she leaned in towards him, kissing him again. He let go of the wheel to answer, she still tasted sweet, and his heart raced. "Yes David, we are for real. I wouldn't have kissed you if I didn't want to, and I do…if you are my boyfriend." She said shyly and moved away from him.

He took over the wheel again and smiled, his heart was warm and this woman next to him finally let her guard down. He loved her so much, from the very moment they met.

"What are you smiling about?" she said, having that same smile on her face.

"Celia…I love you; I always have. Ever since you walked through the office door, I just couldn't stop staring at you. I don't want to freak you out, I don't want you to run away, I just want us to happen, to be like this, like today." He spoke with some concern in his voice.

Celia looked out the car window, this was serious. David loved her. After all this time, he just had this love hidden and never told her.

She sighed quietly: he was a good man, had a 8-year-old daughter, hard worker and was responsible. It was no problem for her that he was a father, since she couldn't have her own children. She met Ally, cute girl, very cheerful. Her mother was a bit complicated though, sometimes called during work and demanded to talk to David or just to drop of the child. Poor Ally with a mother like that, she needed a stable woman to raise her and why couldn't Celia be that woman.

"I…love you too David, I think I also feel the same but never really addressed it. I've always been on my own, thinking maybe that's all I could do, but now, with you. I want this, us."

David stopped the car in the nearest lot, they had to walk for a few minutes to the store, but he just wanted to have her in his arms again. He turned off the engine, turned in his seat towards her and reached for her hands. Celia stretched them towards his and they held on for a few minutes before she pulled him closer to kiss him again. The man was a friggin'magnet!!

"OMG! It's almost 8:30!! We really must go, one more! "Letting him go, got out of the car and waited for him. He came around and grabbed her hand, walking towards the store. If she could tell her middle school boyfriend to sod it, tell her younger self that things will be better, she would.

"I'm going to grab a cart, do you have a list, or you make it up as you go?" he said bringing the cart over to her. She smiled big, took out her phone and showed him a list: "Right here, although I might need some stuff too. Do you want something?"

David grabbed her hand, pulled her close and said, "I have everything I want, right here." He kissed her gently and they went inside.

From afar they looked like this married couple, he rolled the cart, and she checked the list. As they stopped for some sweets, David received a call: "David…yeah, yeah, Tamara hold on a sec. This was supposed to be your week, she's your daughter too! No, no I can't right now. Hey honey, I'm sorry, what? Okay, yeah, I'll pick you up, okay? Okay sweetie, bye."

Celia came back with a bag of bread and saw David's sad eyes: "What is it?" David scratched his head and said "Tamara called; she wants me to pick up Ally earlier because she's having someone over. I'll drop you off and then I'll pick up my daughter."

"Let's pass on our way home, I do want to say hi, poor thing. Maybe she wants some cookies. Come on, let's go." She said and took the cart towards the self-help cashier. He took out his wallet and she put on her card on the reader, teasing him "Too slow!" They laughed, they took one bag each and headed for the car. Left everything in the back end of the car, before driving off.

It was a quiet but happy ride, they stopped at a big building and a small girl with braided hair and a suitcase was standing outside. No mother to be seen.

"Ally, hey honey, how are you?" Celia said and hugged her, the child was very tired, still in her pajamas. "Mom has a visitor; she gave me a paper to daddy. I want to sleep Celi, so tired."

She picked up the girl and carried her to the car, David gave his daughter a kiss and said "I'm going upstairs, wait here." She looked at him with some sadness, this won't end well.

CHAPTER 3:
DAUGHTER INTERRUPTUS

Celia sat back in the car with Ally in her arms, she was sleeping heavily. She took out the phone from her bag and sent a text to her mom: "Hey mom, it's been a delay but I've bought the things we needed and, on my way. David is taking me."

Ally woke up for a minute, she just hugged Celia more and fell asleep again. She kissed her head and kept her close, sleeping was not a bad idea.

When she finally woke up, David was pulling over to her apartment. He smiled, his 2 best girls were together and maybe now they could be a family. "Hey babe, we're here. Want some help?" Celia nodded, she put Ally in the seat with her fluffy bag underneath her head so she could continue resting, gave her a kiss on the forehead and closed the door gently. David got out, helped her with the bags and stopped to give her a long hug: "I'm sorry, I just couldn't take it anymore. She's having some guy over and sends Ally away like she's nothing. I'm going to apply for sole custody, she agrees, says that it would be best if I kept her. I'm just sorry for my baby, she doesn't have a mother who cares enough." He took a deep breath of her shoulder, and she could hear him tearing up.

"Listen, you're doing what's best for Ally, she knows that. And I'm happy to be part of your lives and would be honored to be her bonus mom. I love her, and you." Celia was surprised to talk like that, but it just felt right.

She didn't know that she wanted to be a mom until she met Ally and since they got along well, it wasn't an issue. To support the man, she loved, and his daughter felt natural.

"You and Ally are the most important people in my life, to have you close it's just perfection for me. I love you so much. I'm sorry I can't meet your mother today but there will be other days. I hope. Goodnight honey, talk later?" he said and kissed her goodnight.

He drove off and she entered the building, in the elevator she took out her keys and opened the door on the 7th floor. Mom was sleeping on the sofa, while her sister was watching tv. She jumped out to greet her: "Hey, you're late. What did you bring?"

"Hey, sorry, David's ex-wife just left their daughter on the street. Poor kid was still asleep! Have you eaten?" Celia took out the groceries, washed her hands and left her bag in the bedroom. Claire followed "Yeah we had dinner 2 hours ago, mom wanted something for tomorrow that's because she was in a hurry. Guess the batteries are low ha-ha."

Celia went to get a blanket for mom, she woke up: "Hey, you're home. What time is it?"

"It's after 10, mom, sorry but David had an errand to pick up. He told me to say hi to you." Celia said and took a seat next to her mother. "What happened?"

"Well, his ex-wife turned the child out of the house, because she had a date over. Ally was still asleep while standing in front of their building when we arrived, I put her in the back of the car while waiting for David." Celia said and took a deep breath, something she often did when a lot of questions came.

"His wife shouldn't do that, poor child. Does she know you?" said mom and took a bite of one of the buns Celia brought from the store.

Celia closed her eyes "His ex-girlfriend mom, they've broke up 5 years ago. David is single."

Mom continued "Still, they should've thought about the child. Who's going to raise her if her mother isn't supportive? What is he going to do with her alone?"

Celia got up and went to the kitchen, poured a glass of water and went back inside "He's not alone mom, we're sort of together now. I'm going to help with Ally, she'll be my stepdaughter. She's known me for a long time and we get along, we'll manage."

Mom sat up in the sofa, moved away the blanket and said "How on Earth will you do that? She's not yours, you cannot raise her! Tell David he can forget about it."

Celia was furious! How could she say something like this?

"Uh mom, what are you talking about? Of course, I can, Ally is a bright kid.

We've known each other ever since David began working with us 5 years ago and she loves me! Besides, I'm going to be her stepmom any way since David and I are together, I'm not going to leave him alone."

Mom got up from the sofa, she couldn't accept what I was saying: "I don't think it's a good idea, she needs to be with her mom and dad, not some stranger."

"Mom, this is 2022, we can raise a child together. Besides, I'm going to be supportive of both. You should think about it, this is the closest you're getting to grandchildren on my side." Celia said and headed for her bedroom, mom didn't reply anything.

She picked up her home clothes and went to shower, thinking about what she experienced that day: she had become a girlfriend and a stepmom in one day. Everything was so great, why would mom be so opposed? Celia had been single for 25 years, never dated more than once and was only committed to work and family.

As she got out of the shower, she overheard her mother and sister talking: "Mom, she's 30. You know that she can't have kids of her own? What's wrong with her raising her boyfriends' kid?" Mom said something she couldn't understand, she moved closer to the door but still nothing. She dried herself and got dressed, got out of the bathroom, and proceeded to fix a cup of tea.

"What happens if she wants him back? Will you back away?" mom finally said, looking for somewhat loopholes in her relationship.

"Mom, listen. I don't know what will happen between us. That's for God to decide, and if he doesn't want me, then I'll move on. But I cannot keep thinking that it won't last or that I must wait more time. I have faith in God, that's all I need. "

Mom stared for a while, then she smiled "I'm happy that you're so mature. I'm simply scared that you would get hurt and never recover. I know how you are."

She's like this my mom, cautious almost like a deer. I get why, my father was unfortunately a deadbeat, he had a bunch of kids after me and he just couldn't grow up. I wanted to badly to have my mother find a good guy to marry, to be genuinely happy with but no, she just got another deadbeat after my father. My sisters' father is the same, he only made her unhappy. We suffered a lot with him but somehow, she got the courage to kick him out of the house. He barely has a civil conversation with my sister but mostly just arguments, he always tried to make her do his bidding, but Claire is headstrong and always went against the stream.

She's a good kid, my sister. We're a trio of strong women just looking for some peace.

Celia sat in her room for a while, she was too tired to argue. A little music might cheer her up, so she put on some James Blunt. She thought about what mom said, about her becoming a stepmom to someone else's kid. Could she make a difference in Ally's life?

Mom came in with tea, she sat down next to Celia and said "I'm sorry honey, I don't doubt that you could become a good mother. I think I've never seen anyone so committed to becoming a parent than you, even though you said that you never would have children. You're not your fathers' child, you're mine. Ally will be lucky to have you as her mother."

Celia smiled, mom was a bit erratic sometimes but then she could be so sweet and understanding. A walking contradiction, some would say. But nether less, supportive in times of need or just always. They hugged and said "Okay, now I really think you should watch some of these food channels to learn something new to cook. They went to the living room to sit with mom's husband Fred, they met 6 years ago through work. He was an electrician that came to fix some cables during the remodeling of the dining room in school. She offered him coffee and lunch, they talked about work and suddenly by the end of the week, he just couldn't let her go so he asked her out for lunch.

Fred was almost 62, unmarried, no kids and just lived his life committed to his work. When he met Celia's mom he was smitten beyond reason. She didn't think more of it, but in the end, she had felt quite lonely these past 30 something years. And the man was perfect, he was the man she had needed all her life. He considered us girls his daughters, since he was the best man to be our father, we automatically began calling him dad.

When my sister married her boyfriend Patrick a year ago, he led her to the altar when her own father wasn't even there.

He also cried when she said yes to marry him, since they did their engagement thing at home. When she told the family she was pregnant, he was the first one to run to her to hug her.

"Your mother is worried about you becoming a mother, but I don't. You're going to be a great mom, you were a great one to your sister." I hugged him for that, sat down on my couch and checked the book he was reading: Isabel Allende's "Paula".

Mom smiled and said: "You know, she read that in 4th degree. She has always been a bookworm; reads everything she finds." Fred removed his glasses and said "Well, they take from you…you're smart, beautiful and a hell of a cook! Of course, the girls would be intelligent and funny." Aww my dear mom and my sweet dad, I wish they'd met sooner.

The phone in the bedroom rang, Celia went to check, and it was David: "Hey babe, we're home and the little one is asleep. What are you doing?" She closed the door, sat down on the bed "I was talking to mom and dad oh well Claire too. I told them, that I'm going to become a stepmom to Ally and well that you and I are an item."

Silence in the background, for a moment she thought there was something wrong but suddenly she heard him say "On the phone, hang on. Baby, Ally wants to say something." A tiny voice took over "Halloo? Celli? Hi, thank you for picking me up today!! I love you, goodnight momma." Did she just say? Did she just call me mom??

Tears and more tears came running down her cheeks: "You're more than welcome sweetie, I love you so much my little daughter. Goodnight." David came back and she heard him sniff, he was very emotional about the whole becoming a family thing.

"I love her and you, so much!! I really got to go now, I'm very tired and I'll see you tomorrow at work, okay?" she said, David smirked, Celia could hear him. "I'll pick you up tomorrow, our little girlie will ride along and we'll drop her off at school. Well, goodnight baby, sweet dreams and we love you! Bye, mwah." She hung up, she had her very own family now, if her 14-year-old self would see this, it would be the fairy tale she used to write.

"Mom, pops, off to work now. Later!" "Bye hon, take care!" mom and dad said while she closed the door. Celia locked the door, took the elevator, and went to the entrance. There he was, David and little Ally sitting in the back. She opened the door and ran out to hug me "Celli!!!!! How are you momma?" I grabbed her in my arms, we hugged, and I went to the car with her. "Hi baby, how are you?" David said, while I was helping Ally with the security belt. Celia gave him a quick kiss before strapping herself next to her in the back. They drove off to her school, helped her out and each of them took a hand to walk her to the front door.

"Bye honey, love you and we'll pick you up after school. Give me a hug, one for your dad. Bye!" Celia said and she hugged them both, she's the sweetest kid. Some people use the term "salt of the earth", Celia would say sugar.

"So, just us now. What should we do, it's more than an hour to start work?" He said while she was getting in the car, front seat. Ha-ha, he was always looking for more. Was it just me or were we both a little too hot lately? For a moment, her anxiety was giving her a hard time. David put his hand om Celia's knee "Are you okay? You look slightly pale. Did you eat breakfast? Do you want something?"

She woke up from her short coma, just nodded and said "Nah, on y va". David pulled her close to kiss her, but there was something more in his kiss today, like need or something stronger. "Whoa hey, are you okay now?" Celia said with some concern in her voice.

David pulled back, he felt ashamed or something similar because he only stared at the window. She put her hand on his chest, to show support for his feelings and he grabbed it to kiss it. "I'm sorry, it's just that I have this need for having you close. I want to spend some time alone with you but not here, how about we play hooky today and just go to a hotel? I want…with you."

"Wait, what? Did he just propose to sleep together? We've known each other a long time though, supported each other during tough times. We weren't strangers to each other, so it's not entirely weird but gosh it feels so different. I think this is the moment my friend Paolo told me about "Will you be ready to be with a man when that moment comes?" I was nervous but not in a bad way, not like before when another guy suggested in right after their first date. It felt normal, just like when his daughter called me momma, David was the one I wanted to be with for the rest of my life." Celia thought to herself.

"Yes, I want to. Let me call work first." She said, sounded more than attractive since David had this fire in his eyes. "Yeah, hi Bert, it's me. I'm fine thanks and you? Listen I need a favor, I need to take a personal day. That's what personal means Bert, oh and it's not just for me, yeah David. No nothing like that, we are working stuff out and to do so we need to have some time. Don't worry, we'll be there tomorrow. Thanks Bert, you're the best. I'll check emails during the day. Okay thanks, bye."

Celia bit her lip, David was insanely gorgeous in his grey suit, with white shirt and just as grey vest and for some reason she just wanted to rip it off. "Where to?" she said, and he drove off.

They arrived at this beautiful hotel a little outside of Birmingham, they didn't say a word on the whole ride there. Just a bunch of lustful eye contact, smiles and before getting out of the car a deep kiss. Now this one was different; it was more tender than the needy/lusty one before. "Mm, I want to keep kissing you forever and still it won't be enough." He said before grabbing her hand and went to the hotel; Celia saw the sign on the door "5 star and Gordon Ramsay's menu". Wow this was fancy, maybe too fancy for her ordinary jeans and t-shirt with green light jacket.

"Ehh maybe this is too fancy, I don't think I can. Maybe we could go some other place." She said and stopped a few meters from the door. David grabbed her waist and said "Hey, you're perfect and I wouldn't share this with anyone else. Come on."

They went inside, there was this concierge speaking French on the phone. Suddenly it felt like the "French Kiss" scene, where Kate rang the bell. "Hi, reservation for David Castle." The concierge checked the computer, he said that the room was available until tomorrow midday. He paid and whispered something in his ear. "Certainly, sir, please, room 566, 5th floor. Charlie, please escort our guests to the 5th floor. Here's your keycard sir. If you need any more assistance my name is Luc Letellier. Madam." He nodded towards them, and she smiled, they didn't bring any luggage but the bellhop accompanied them to the elevator.

"5th floor ma'am, sir. We hope you enjoy your stay." He said and left them outside the door to the room. "Thank you." David said and gave the young guy a £5 bill, he turned to Celia and said, "Will you do me the honors?" She took the keycard and entered the room.

It was beautiful! The interior, the flowers, it was an apartment! Interesting that most of it had her favorite colors: lilac in different shades. By the bedside table lied a tiny box in a very known shade of turquoise… Wait, Tiffany's? Was this?

"I had this planned for some time, I thought it would take longer but since we are where we are I thought this is as good time as any. Celia Andrea Caceres, will you do me the extremely honor of being my wife? I promise to love you endlessly, to be faithful in all ways, support every move you make and to make you happy forever. This is all of me and I want all of you." He said and kneeled; Celia just stood there with the box in her shaky hands.

He proposed, it's been 2 days, how can he possibly?

"I, I don't know what to say. David are you sure? Is this really what you want? Because you know, we can wait." She said and sat down on the perfect bed, David got up and sat next to her. "Listen, I don't care how long we wait to get married. In my heart, we already are. You accepted my daughter and me in your life and that's more than enough. This ring, it's just a formality. A rock as a token of what you are to us, more beautiful of course but a pilar in our lives. You know, I asked Ally to help me? She knew this was perfect for you. We don't have to plan anything yet, when you see fit, that's when."

Celia took a deep breath; she was in shock.

CHAPTER 4:
ANSWERS

The room service came with strawberries, nonalcoholic champagne, and chocolate, she was standing by the window admiring the view. David came over with a glass and a small plate of strawberries, he gave it to her, and she picked one. He put the plate down on the table, next to the ring box. As he put his arms around her waist, nuzzling her left cheek with his nose he whispered "Well this isn't so bad right? Maybe we should think about moving here, find a nice house close to the lake, big room for Ally and if you want, we could get a dog or a cat?"

Celia turned her face towards his, she didn't want to talk anymore. A hunger for kissing him with a slight restraint, as she held his face in her hands careful to not scratch him with her newly engagement ring. She took it off and put it on the table.

She kissed him again and he sighed; she could tell he wanted more than just kiss. She pushed him onto the bed and to his happy surprised face removed his jacket and vest, his shirt smelled of Burberry Brit and one by one removed the buttons leaving his chest bare. He's a very good-looking man, Celia's future husband. He sat up and lifted her shirt, kissed her not so flat stomach that made her laugh, he kept his face there while holding her waist and moved his hands to her butt. He pulled her down, this time he was on top. Celia had never been stripped by anyone before, it felt good though, maybe because she loved and felt loved by him. David was careful, gentle, and sweet. It did hurt though; it was her first time.

He knew that, but still she felt safe. It was a whole new experience and for someone who had nothing to compare with, he was the best. It was almost like he could hear her thoughts because he asked "Are you okay? Did I hurt you?" They kissed and he held her in his arms until she fell asleep, she could hear him whisper "I love you."

Sunshine in the face, it had to be late afternoon. He was asleep by her side, Celia couldn't help but smile. The big clock in the room showed 14:30 in the afternoon, Ally should get off school in an hour. She got up, found a silky robe on the chair. She guessed something he bought in advance. Celia went to his side, kissed him gently on the lips and whispered "Hey sleepy head, we have to go. Ally is getting off school and no one can pick her up." He answered that kiss by pulling her robe towards him, he still smelled of Burberry. She couldn't help but bury her face in his neck and he laughed, she didn't know he was ticklish. "Hello honey, don't worry. I asked your parents to pick her up, we're staying until tomorrow morning before work. A preview of the honeymoon and it's looking mighty fine so far."

"So, wait, what are we supposed to do until tomorrow then?" she said with a cheeky, seductive smile. He laughed "Hahaha no no, no more of the good stuff. We're having dinner and then, we're going to the hotels dancing night. You need to practice for our wedding dance." He closed her robe, tried to reach for his but Celia stopped him "Can't dinner wait?".

They had an exquisite lovemaking moment; it would seem she was getting a grip of it or that he just couldn't let go of her. "That was incredible, we could just stay in bed you know until hm next year?" She laughed "No no sir, you did say that we're going dancing later. Celia had never danced before, well not as an adult just when she was in kindergarten when she was 5. "I'm not even sure I can dance anymore."

He sat up, kissed her bare shoulder. It was like electricity going through her, she moved his arm towards her waist and turned a bit to reach his lips. Much more intense than before, they were like magnets unable to let each other go. "Baby, take a shower with me." He whispered under his breath, taking her hand, and leading her to the bathroom. Celia couldn't resist him, his perfectly chiseled body was almost like an Adonis from Greece. He turned on the shower and pulled her in, they kissed for a while. He nibbled gently on her earlobe and I couldn't stop laughing, he tried to move away the water from her face and said "I love you so much Celia, I didn't think I ever could be this happy. You and Ally are everything to me." Celia didn't know if he had tears in his eyes or if it was just the water from the shower but she did feel his concern. "Hey, listen to me. I love you and Ally; you mean so much to me and nothing is going to change that. Now, I really need a towel or we'll end up raisins skin."

David laughed, got out from the shower, and got a towel from the rack. He put one around his waist and got a bigger one to wrap her with, he kissed her nose and said "I'll find one for your hair."

As he walked out from the bathroom, Celia realized how lucky she was, to have such a good man in her life. Her short hair was drying satisfactory, and she just admired him from the doorway. Walked closer to wrap her arms around his waist, he gave her a big smile and turned around. "Want to go back to the shower or bed?" She shut him up in a kiss, they really needed to get some clothes on and have something to eat. They got dressed in each other's presence, he admired her and when she caught him, he blushed. She did the same, but didn't blush, it wasn't awkward between them, just love. He was finalizing with his white shirt when Celia felt the urge to help him, he let her. She wanted to feel his skin under her fingers, to feel his strong arms, to caress his back and realized he had scars on either shoulder blade. He flinched when she touched them "What happened?" He took her hand towards his chest and said "Old scars, accident when I was a teenager. Nothing to worry about."

Celia moved my hand towards the scars, it would seem like burn marks. "Tell me, who did this to you?"

He sat down with her in his lap, he pushed his face towards her neck and said "Remember when I told you I was adopted? Well, I was in foster care for 5 years. My pre-teens where a nightmare, it wasn't until I was 14 when the Castle's adopted me that I felt safe, you know. Normally people don't adopt older kids but the Castles were simply perfect, I still miss them. They would have been happy to meet you and Ally now, she was just a baby when they died. Well, when I was 12 there was this kid in my class, a real bully. Anthony, I still remember his dark evil eyes. Well, he and 2 others hang me from my shoulder blades in the gym. You know those rings you can work out with? They had these small hooks, since they couldn't put them in the skin, they burned the hook. Painful, but I got help and counseling after that, nobody besides my parents and now you have seen them. Tamara didn't even bother to look, I guess she didn't care enough."

Celia couldn't help it, her eyes were flooding with tears. How could someone endure such pain and still be a loving human being? She held him towards her, caressed his scars and got up from his lap. She took his hands, have him standing in front of her and just gave him a hug. He kissed her head and whispered "Knowing that you're here with me is more than enough. The past is just that Celia, past. I don't feel that pain anymore because God gave me so much more to live for, that is a reward for me.

What if I had been taught never to love anyone? Now, everything we've been through together...it was worth the pain."

Celia smiled, he truly was a heaven-sent man...a good father, a good boyfriend/fiancée/lover everything a woman could wish for. She couldn't resist him, they kissed, and she unbuckled his pants, apparently, he couldn't resist her either, she pushed in onto the bed and whispered, "Roll over". He didn't understand what she had in mind but just to have him on his belly (the one he didn't have) and kiss his back, his scarred shoulder blades and then back on his lips. He sighed, it was satisfaction for him, to be this open with Celia, tell her his past demons and to let her address those once fearful moments he lived.

Maybe they shouldn't go to the dance, just stay like that but he was almost done, and she was still in her robe. He went to the closet by the window and pulled out a beautiful chiffon dress in black, with black ballerinas (he knew she hated high heels). "This is for today; it will match the ring perfectly. I'll wear the white shirt and the black pants, no jacket or with jacket?" Celia was in another world, she just wanted him to be bare chest at her mercy but said "Jacket, I want to remove that later. It's beautiful, thank you honey." He smiled, watched as she got dressed and helped her with the zipper. "Shall we, Mrs. Castle?"

The salon was big, lots of flowers and this huge lamp. Lot of people mingling, David approached the bartender and he said "Hi, reservation for Castle plus one?" "Of course, Mr. Castle this way please. Here's the wine list and the menu, Carla will be your waitress today. I'll give you a moment to decide."

They sat down, he waited for her to sit first and poured some water in a glass. She checked the menu, never drank wine or anything like that, she liked her drinks virgin.

"Grilled entrecote with mashed potatoes and greens, gravy. Think I can exchange the mashed for fries? I don't like my things mashed or overcooked…feels like purée." Celia told him and he couldn't hold the laughter, it seemed like she was very amusing. He was caressing her leg with his shoe; She gave him a small kick and he blushed. "Waitress please, yeah 2 grilled entrecotes with greens, no mash but fries. Oh, and a pitcher of peach iced tea. Thank you." "Certainly, sir, ma'am." said the waitress and took the menus.

"It's beautiful here, I think I've heard of this place but never been. How come you chose it?" she said taking a sip of the water, he smiled and took her hand, the one with the ring. "Because my fiancée deserves it, to be honest, I checked the same night you accompanied me to pick up Ally. I checked at home and made the reservations on standby; I knew you would say yes to the proposal." He looked so smug; it was his plan all along. "But how, remember that we were supposed to fake it so they would leave me alone. Or was that your plan all along?" she said, it was confusing though. Now there was fear in his eyes, if she had said no, he would just wait until she said yes?

"Listen baby, I knew there was some uncertainty from your side. I mean that I was willing to wait until you decided to be with me, because I've loved you all this time. Ever since you walked in the office as a trainee therapist, your smile, your red cheeks and mostly your kindness. I had never met anyone with a purer soul than yours, any amount of time with you is valuable. I wanted you to be sure." He kept her hand on his and moved his thumb to caress hers, she smiled, and it really was difficult to pretend she didn't feel the same. He was the only one who cared for real, who wanted to know her. "Then cheers, for us and the future." she said and clinked her glass with his. The dinner had not arrived when she said "I'm just going to the bathroom, I'll be right back."

Celia took her purse and went towards the bar, asking "Excuse me, where's the bathroom?" The bartender showed her, towards the elevators on the left. Instead of going into the bathroom, she took the elevator to their floor. Since the concierge gave them a set of keys, she kept one in her purse. Celia entered and undressed, found her casual clothes, and left both dress, shoes, and engagement ring on the bed. She found a piece of paper and wrote "I'm sorry, I can't do this." closed the door and headed for the elevator, went to the front desk to a tall woman behind the computer. "Miss, can you get me a taxi to central Birmingham? Train station is fine." "Of course, ma'am." It had been approximately 10 minutes since she went to the "bathroom", hopefully he hadn't noticed anything yet.

The taxi arrived and she said, "Birmingham central please."

Celia went home, thinking about what she had done. The love was there but somehow, she feared that it wouldn't be enough. Was it enough to last a lifetime? She did not want to make any mistakes or more specific: she did not want to get hurt. It was pointless to continue the relationship, of course she loved him but if he ever left, how could she cope? The pain and suffering, she could do that on her own.

David had called 2 times already, but she kept clicking off the phone. A voicemail blinked on the screen, but she pressed 5 and deleted without listening. Instead, she dialed her father's number: "Hey dad it's me, I need a favor. Could you meet me at Birmingham airport with my suitcase and some money? Yeah no, don't tell mom. Is Ally there? Okay, no don't tell her I'm here. Thanks, see you in 20 minutes. Love you!"

At the hotel bar, David tried calling Celia several times. Nothing, he got worried that something had happened. Suddenly like a flash from the sky, he went back to the room and found her dress, ring, and a note. The note that broke his heart.

"What happened? Did he hurt you?" Dad said while hugging Celia tight, she nodded and explained what happened with the proposal. He looked at her with some concern but comforted her that her decisions were just that: hers.

"Don't worry, I'm sure you'll find the correct answers. He's coming to pick up the girl, want me to tell him anything? He's going to be worried you know, maybe he deserves the truth."

She had tears in her eyes, maybe it was wrong to leave him like this, but she felt cornered and needed to get away. "No dad, thanks. You don't know what happened to me or where I am, we'll just leave it at that. I got to go, thank you daddy, for this and everything you do for our family. I love you." Celia said and gave him one last hug, he grabbed her hand and put a money pouch in it. "Dad…" "No Celia, I know you need some money just in case. I don't want you to have problems wherever you're going. Promise me that you will take care of yourself and call as soon as you arrive." He said, Celia could tell that he was worried but wanted to support her in any way. She left him there and mouthed "I love you!" before entering Birmingham International. As she walked through the airport, she stopped and this B&B. "Hi, do you have a room available until tomorrow?" The concierge said yes, and she paid for the room, entered, connected the laptop to the internet and typed: flighttickets.com, one way to London, tomorrow morning. A cheap hotel room for 2 nights was booked, and she took a quick shower before she checked the phone again: 10 missed calls, all from David and about 15 messages. All asked: are you okay, did something happen, did I do something, why don't you pick up, please call me and finally: I love you.

She couldn't deal with him, so she texted to her boss: "Hey Bert, I need a big favor. I need to work from London for some time and you need to tell David that I quit. I was wondering if you know anyone that has an apartment to rent? You're the only one that knows I'm working from London, let's keep it that way. Let me know, thanks."

Short minutes after "Hey, yeah my niece has an apartment that no one uses. Take it, no rent nor problem. U need anything, you call/text or email me. God speed/ B." I got the number for his niece so I would call her as soon as I arrived in London.

She fell asleep on the comfy bed but had a terrible anxiety while thinking about David.

The following morning, she woke up early to take the early flight to London Heathrow, it was about an hour long so no trouble staying awake. She did however need to contact the boss's niece about the apartment. A sleepless flight before landing in London, Celia bought a train ticket to Victoria to then take the subway to Shepherds Bush.

London was a breath of fresh air, it felt so good to be here again. She took the bus to the hotel, not far from where she was standing. Checked in and left the bag on one side of the room, washed her hands to look for some clean clothes. A clean bathroom, something Celia always looked for during her vacations, turned on the shower with almost cold water and took a refreshing shower. The phone rang but she didn't bother to pick it up, instead she wrapped herself in a big towel and sat on the toilet lid. She sighed deeply and remembered the exquisite day in the hotel with David, the remembered his touch that felt like electricity through her body. Maybe this runaway thing was a mistake, she should have explained to him that it felt weird to marry so quickly. Although he said that they would be engaged for as long as she wanted to, so why was this so problematic?

It wasn't David that didn't love her enough, maybe it was her? She made the thoughts disappear, she wouldn't let him touch her if she didn't feel anything!

Celia checked the phone, messages from David again: "Hi Celia, it's me again. Um please, please call me back, I need to talk to you. I need to hear from you what happened. I went to pick up Ally yesterday and asked your dad about you, he did not want to talk to me. Tell me, what did I do? How can I fix it? I love you, call me."

She sighed again, somehow, she felt like a coward. Why couldn't she tell him that it was going to quickly? A scene from "Eat, Pray, Love" came to mind, Julia Roberts screaming to Javier Bardem that he could shove his "darling this and darling that". That's exactly how she's feeling right now, what about what she wanted to do with her life besides getting married? Celia still wanted to travel, do something else besides her regular hours as a therapist. She got up, throwed the phone on the bed and picked up the hotel room phone. Dialed the number to her boss's niece, a voice on the other end "This is Alva, hi Celia, yeah my uncle told me you're in London. Now? Sure, I'm available. The Ibis in Hammersmith got it! See you in 15 minutes. Yeah, bye."

She dressed quickly and closed the door; the air was fresh, and it felt like a good way to start the day. The walk towards Lakeside Road was calm, but all she thought about was walking here with David and Ally. There were the tears again, she wiped them off and saw a girl with long hair looking at her watch. "Alva?"

Celia said and the girl smiled, they exchanged pleasantries and began walking a few meters to a cute building.

The apartment was on the first floor and was very spartanly equipped: hallway, kitchen, bathroom, toilet, bedroom, and a tiny balcony. It was perfect, to be my first apartment. "I haven't signed up for internet yet and since I'll be working from here for the time being, I'm going to check with the company." Celia said and discovered a little box that said Virgin Media. "Oh, this house already has, since no one ever used it, we only pay like £10 extra a month. Feel free to use it. Did you bring a laptop?" She nodded and they continued the tour, deciding to have some coffee. "You can move in whenever you want, if you need anything or help, let me know. My husband and I moved here from Leeds, left all our friends there so I don't really know many people. Oh, and his friend is looking for a nice girl, maybe you could hit it off?"

Celia gave her a weak smile "Thanks but I just left a relationship. I'll stay on my own for now but I'll be happy to have you guys over for dinner and so once I settle in. Thank you, Alva, for everything." They parted ways and Celia went back to the hotel, to get some sleep again. Food was out of the question, but she knew she needed to eat. She grabbed her wallet, checked if there was enough money but left the phone. Headed out the door, to the closest Prêt a Manger and bought a noodle salad with beef. They had fruit in these little containers, she took one as well. A bottle of ice-cold tea and then back to the hotel.

There was news on tv, but no movies until 5 pm. After the tiny late lunch, Celia took a nap. Everything came to mind: she missed David, kept dreaming about their first night together mixed with the guilt of running away. She also saw the future, or so she thought: It must have been a long time, because when she saw him again, Ally, his daughter was about 15 now. He had married someone else; a blonde woman and they were happy, she heard Ally call her mom. David was just as she knew him, except now he had a wedding band on his left ring finger. He didn't stop to say hi, in fact none of them stopped.

She woke up, it was now 7:30 pm. Mom had called twice, left just a simple text message "Are you okay? Why didn't you tell me you were going to London? Call me, love you!"

Then it was one from David "I'm downstairs, please just talk to me." Wait? He was here?? Celia got dressed quickly and went downstairs, no David to be seen, then she felt a hand on her shoulder "Celi…" That voice, she could recognize it anywhere… David. She turned around, there he was in a white shirt and suit pants. His Burberry Brit aftershave surrounded him, and she felt the electricity in her body. Before they kissed, she woke up again.

It had been a dream, just a dream. She checked the time, it was now 6:45 pm and she realized how much that man meant to her. Celia wanted to call him but didn't manage to dial his number, come to think of it, the phone had no messages and no missed calls anymore, maybe he got tired of it now. Instead, she called her dad "Hey dad it's me. Everything is okay, I'm at the hotel and tomorrow I'll be moving to Lakeside Road. No dad, I'm not going back for now. Tell mom I said hi and tell Claire that I'll text her. Love you dad, bye."

CHAPTER 5:
WITH NO BEGINNING,
THERE'LL BE NO END

Breakfast time at the hotel the following morning was splendid, she was quite hungry after last night. Now Celia was making a list of things she needed for the apartment, a bedside lamp will be good, a small tv and a DVD player.

Today was all about getting stuff ready for the new home, for a moment she was getting cold feet…that home should've been both David's and hers. But she needed to continue with her life, he needed at least that from her even though it broke her heart. She grabbed her bag and headed out the door, walked outside and took the bus to central London. A visit to Primark, Argos, Victoria's Secret, HMW and finally Prêt a Manger for some noodle salad. She passed outside Tiffany's on her way home in Westfield Mall (close to Waitrose) and remembered the ring that David had bought her. "I'm sorry" she thought to herself and kept walking, when suddenly someone grabbed her hand.

"Excuse me ma'am but I think you dropped this" a man said with a voice that could be recognized anywhere. David was standing there, right there. Celia felt her knees tremble and dropped some of her bags. "Hi Celia…so this is where you've been hiding from me." It was sad tone in his voice, she knew that she hurt him badly with her running away, but it would hurt more if she had stayed.

"David, I'm sorry. I needed to get away, I never meant to hurt you." She said and recovered the bags he was now holding. They found a bench by the entrance, sat down and he had tears in his eyes. "Why can't you be with me? Is it the marriage thing? I told you it's just a formality, we don't have to get married now. It's to show how much I love you and that I want you to be my wife one day." He said trying to touch her hands, but she kept moving away. "He stopped trying and kept the hands to himself, Celia didn't want to comfort him because it could mean they could end up together. "I'm sorry David, I know it's hard for you to understand but I can't do this. I can't be in a relationship because I come from a messed-up family. Even though my mom did everything to keep us out of it, my stepdad screwed with my head and I just can't remove it. What I felt, it will never go away. I thought time could be helpful but it doesn't. I'm sorry, look I need to go." She said and stood up, barely looked at him "Goodbye David, I hope you find the woman of your dreams. She's out there, I know it." David stood up and held out his hand, she took it and then left.

Back at the apartment, she left the bags on the floor and went to the kitchen to get a cup of tea. It had been shocking to see David again, she had dreamt of their "reunion" in so many ways but this one was truly painful. She knew that this, it would never go away. After David she would never date again.

The TV arrived at last, she was working in the small living room when the door rang. She peeked through the peephole and there was a man with a package in his hand, opened the door and asked "Yes?" The man was a bit weird, like he was nervous or something. "Uh hello ma'am, are you miss Celia? There's a package for you. Sign here please?" She signed and thanked him, closed the door. Apart from the TV, there was nothing else she was about to receive. She opened carefully; it was from David. A tearful sigh when she saw a frame with their picture together, a picture they took when they first met. She smiled; it was almost 6 years ago during a visit to London Zoo.

With it a letter, handwritten, the ones she loved best. Celia was almost afraid to read it.

Dear Celia,
I'm sorry to barge in here in your "safe" place but I needed to ask what happened since we last saw each other? I know it hasn't been long but it was too long for me.
Did I say something wrong? Is it the marriage thing? Just tell me, you can't hurt me more than leaving things unsaid. I know you said messed-up family but look what you've accomplished together! What you did for Ally, I'll never forget that and she adores you. I'll stay in London for a week, Ally's with my brother and his wife. I'm staying at the Ibis in Victoria, you can call me whenever. If not, well I guess this would be the end of it. I'm not going to force you into something you don't want to be in but if you need time, I can give it to you. Just tell me, talk to me.
I'll love you until the day you tell me to leave and even if you do, I'll love you in silence.
Take care,
With love
David

She was so sad now; the TV assembly went straight to hell after this letter. The tissue box was on the table, and she grabbed one, without hesitation she wanted to call him and tell him that they should try again but she also knew that it would be problematic to feel the same thing again: the pain in her heart, the feel of going through what her mom did, the frightening feeling of loving someone too much and to lose herself in the process.

But David never demanded anything, he was not that kind of guy: he was funny, intelligent, thoughtful, sweet. A dream guy in all aspects.

Maybe she got this the wrong way, the person demanding was Celia herself. She forgot that David wasn't her stepfather or her deadbeat father: he was a responsible father to his daughter.

She tried to imagine their life together, him making dinner in the kitchen, just being a dork really. Celia smiling from the couch, filming him to show him how dorky he was. Dancing together in the living room, spending time with Ally and their families. It was a normal life, no worries in sight except her own worries, her ghosts from past experiences. Maybe even David's ex but not even she was an issue.

Celia went to the kitchen, stared out the curtainless window to the street outside. A few people walking, buses driving and some birds singing. Then she heard those words again, a well know song "With no beginning, there will be no end". What if the song needed to be interpreted differently?

"Enough of the psychoanalysis, call him or don't. Your

call." She thought to herself, picked up the phone and dialed David's number.

One ring "Hey, I'm glad you called. How are you?" he said, and she could hear him smile. "Hey, I um, I didn't want to leave things just like that. Can you come over?" Celia said, biting her lip. "Sure, where are you staying? Uh, yeah, I can be there in 20 minutes. I'll call you when I'm outside so you can let me in. See you then, bye."

She cleaned up, washed her face, and waited for him to arrive. He called: "Hi, I'm outside now. Code? Okay, thanks." He knocked quietly on her door, she looked out and saw him, opened the door. David thought he was dreaming having her close again. A tiny smile escaped her lips and she moved to the side to let him in. He was wearing black pants, a blue t-shirt, and a grey sweater over his shoulders. She could tell that he was nervous, his lower lip trembled a bit and all she could think of was how badly she wanted to kiss him again. He scratched his head lightly, like trying to figure out what was going on in her mind. She pushed him away and now it would seem she wanted him back?

"Nice apartment, yours?" he said, looking around through the hall. She smiled and gestured towards the living room/kitchen, he sat down on the sofa, and she kept a distance in a chair. They looked at each other for a while, David was trying to hide is enthusiasm but couldn't much longer. Celia smiled answering "No it belongs to Bert's niece, I'm borrowing it for the time being." He silenced a chuckle; it was very her in many ways: everything in order, in a few days she had made her own home here. Maybe there was no room for him anymore. "Well, I just wanted to uh…talk about what happened earlier today. I wasn't ready to face you or talk about what happened with us back home, but after seeing you today I realized something." She began and kept looking at her hands, David was much more relaxed now but there was something in his eyes…

"I've been thinking about what you said, maybe you're right. I shouldn't have continued with this when I realized you didn't love me. So, I'll make it easy for both of us…I'm letting go." Celia was confused, his voice was like never: disappointment, some anger but also sadness. She responded: "If this is what you want, I won't stop you. Maybe it will be for the best, a chance for you to find what you really need." Her lips formed a line, within she was already crying. But wasn't this what she wanted all along? For him to let her go.

David gave her a weak smile, walked towards her, and stretched out his hand. She took it and he held on to it for a short moment, before heading out the door.

Celia closed it behind him, went back to the living room. Tears overflowing her eyes and she couldn't breathe anymore.

CHAPTER 6:
THE YEARS, HAVE BEEN KIND.

4 years later, Celia was back in Birmingham. Her sister had just delivered her second baby and she had become an aunt to a little boy: Max.

The flight was quick, she kept the earphones all the way until baggage claim at Birmingham International. During this time living in London, her family had visited her, but she never went back home. Scared she might run into David, she invited them over instead, now she was finally ready to face whatever. Her father was waiting by the entrance, she shouted "Daddyoooo" and jumped into his arms. He held on to her for a while, before letting her down gently "Hey kiddo, how was the flight?" They spoke for a while walking out of the airport into his car. She was eager to ask about David but kept holding on to the question until Fred said, "David is not here, you can stop fidgeting." Celia turned red; he knew her so well. "Is he on vacation?"

Her father gave her a soft smile, he didn't want to hurt her but, in the end, truth would come out sooner or later. "I'm sorry Celia, he left the UK 2 years ago with his daughter. He now lives in New York and works for the State Department as a consultant, he came to say goodbye you know. I think hoping you had come home, he left this." He handed her over an envelope with a long letter, she read it in the car, quietly.

"Dad, stop the car. I don't feel so good." She said, he parked by break place, and she got out quickly.

There it was again, the feeling that she couldn't breathe. "I can't, I can't..." she cried out and her father went to her side. "I'm sorry honey, I knew this would only hurt you, but your mother insisted on me giving it to you now. He's not alone, he's dating the DA's daughter since about 1 ½ years now…they're…getting married in November. There's nothing you can do." Celia felt her head spin, but she stayed put and in between cries said, "I know, I made him do this and now he's truly gone."

She went back to the car, put the letter back in the envelope and put it under the car seat. Come to think of it, she never finished the letter. They arrived home and mom came to the door to greet her; Claire was in the living room with her husband and now 2 kids. Little Max Manzani was the cutest kid. Celia had a certain regret of never becoming a mom, her only chance was when David asked her to be his daughters' mom, but we know that never happened. Claire smiled, handed the baby over to Celia and she held him warmly in her arms. Max slept quietly in her arms and she couldn't help but cry a little, Patrick, Claire's husband took the baby while she wiped her tears. "He's beautiful, both your kids Claire. You're a great mom, well parents… I'm happy for you!" Patrick gave her a hug and stood by his wife; it was pure devotion right there just as the first day the met.

Celia went to her bedroom, changed clothes, and just laid there. David's letter was still under the car seat in her father's car but she couldn't continue reading it to know that he was ready to love someone else and she still couldn't move on.

2 weeks after her visit, it was time to fly home to London. This time she said her goodbyes before leaving and took the bus to the airport shuttle. An hour later she was having tea at Marks & Spencer at the airport and the following hour she was already home in her flat in central London. Celia worked during the following months from home until her vacations in July, she bought a ticket to the US but not New York, instead she went to Hawaii.

Ala Moana Avenue was crowded, in a good way. She was finally living her best life, doing what she always wanted and trying to mend her chronical broken heart. The hotel was gorgeous, by the coastline and she could spend all day by the beach doing absolutely nothing. But she did, she signed up for a trekking walk in the mountains, she visited Kilauea and stood by it's feet where she shouted that she was free. Also did a bit of shopping, more sightseeing and got a traditional tattoo by a Samoan citizen: a hibiscus flower on her shoulder blade. Hurt like hell but worth it.

A sunny morning, she went surfing and met some nice people, they invited her to a luau in the evening. It was a beautiful party with loads of people, music, and dancing. Oh, the dancing, well she did some of that with a local guy: Steve. He was native Hawaiian with an English mother. They became good friends while her vacation, he had a house in LA and told her if she ever wanted to come by, she was welcome.

The next day she was going for a scuba lesson when she got a not so nice surprise: the DA's daughter was just getting of the rental car, and she was not alone: David was with her. Her heart skipped a beat: he looked even more gorgeous than before. They didn't see her, she managed to stay out of the way but at the front desk trying to get her keycard a voice said "Celia?" She froze hearing David's voice, but turned around "David, wow, fancy seeing you here. How's it?" He was appalled by seeing her after 4 years, she looked so much different than the last time: her hair was shorter, black with blue highlights, she looked refreshed and happy. She was more beautiful than ever; on the other hand, she had always been beautiful. His smile was contagious, she felt her heart drop to the ground but kept her smile to a minimum to his disappointment. "I'm fine, you look splendid. How come?" he began when an annoyed voice said "Erm…hi I'm Kayla Jones, and you are?"

Celia turned her eyes to his new girlfriend or better said fiancée, she faked a smile and said "Hi, I'm Celia. Former co-worker of David's. Nice to meet you, well both of you. If you'll excuse me, I have some things to do today. Later." She nodded to them before getting back to her business which was scuba diving.

It was a good day though, she learned a lot and thought about staying in Hawaii for some time. She could have online sessions with her patients, prescribe medication if needed and to stay away from David until he got married to miss DA's stuck up daughter.

Back at the hotel she was ordering some room service when the concierge gave her a message paper. David wanted to see her, if possible, at 10 pm by the pool.

By the time maybe he was waiting until his fiancée was asleep. She told the concierge that she didn't want to leave any messages to him and went to her room, hanged the "Do not disturb" sign on the door to be left alone.

Celia took a quick shower while waiting for the food to arrive. A knock was heard, and she opened in her bathrobe, there was the food and David. It looked like he had bribed the delivery guy to get access to her room, he stood there with a white napkin in his hand "Can we call a truce? I just want to talk." She sighed and let him in.

He sat by the window while she changed clothes in the bathroom, came out and sat on the bed feeling just annoyed. "Tell me, what's going on?" David met her eyes and she saw that he had tears in his eyes, something she couldn't stand because after 4 years, she still loved him. He wiped his tears, chuckled and said "I thought I never would see you again, that I could move on from everything, thinking that I could be happy and here you are. It's like you never left." She was even more annoyed, so it was her fault that he moved across the globe with someone with a good status just to forget about her.

"I'm sorry that you feel that way, but I'm not responsible for what you did during these 4 years. Now if you'll excuse me, I have some things to do besides dinner. Go back to your fiancée, I'm sure she's worried." Celia said with a sourness in her voice.

David got up from the chair and walked towards the door, Celia went to the bathroom to hang her towel when David came back towards her quickly and grabbed her towel, dropping it on the floor.

Before she could say anything, he grabbed her waist and kissed her violently. She kicked him in the balls and pushed him to the floor, what David didn't know that she had been taking kendo classes and was very much into martial arts.

"Oh my…why did you kick me?" he said groaning, grabbing his parts. She chuckled, helped him up and responded "I didn't give you permission to kiss me David, I'm not your girlfriend anymore. And, even if you think I don't feel anything having you close, you're wrong. I never stopped loving you and not a day goes by that I don't miss you. But that is me, my feelings." David was standing now, he pulled her closer and this time, she didn't kick him. They kissed, just as the first time: gentle, sweet and that electric wire that went through both.

"You need to go, you're an engaged man. I can't have that on my conscience." She said and David gave her a sweet sigh, he held her face close to his and whispered, "I love you, I'll end this today and we can go back to the way before." She pulled away, but couldn't let him go. He hugged her, long and hard. Her nose was on his shoulder, he didn't smell of Burberry anymore but Calvin Klein. Another favorite.

Before heading out the door, he took her hand and said "I've stayed faithful to you for these past 4 years, you know. I've never slept with Kayla, told her I wanted to wait but, in a way, I've always waited for you. It never passed kissing her and truth be told, I turned off my feelings because I felt nothing. You're the only one that can provoke me, make me feel complete and the only one I truthfully love."

"But how did you propose to her?" Celia said, slightly confused. "I didn't, she did to sleep with me. So yeah, I'm still yours." David looked so satisfied to get it all out, she smiled, gave him a kiss, and said "Go, goodnight." He laughed a little and left.

Celia was packing her bags; it was time to leave beautiful Hawaii for foggy London. She had spoken to David a few times during her stay, but they decided not to see each other, out of respect for the other partner. He had spoken to his former fiancée, told her that he wanted to call of the wedding, and she agreed. They still had to come to terms for the living arraignments, she had some stuff in his apartment in NY, but she said that he could FedEx them to her. Kayla didn't ask him if there was someone else, but she had felt something weird when she met Celia that time. Except that, she thought David was a little too calm for her, she was after all a NY socialite, and he was more "stay home and watch tv" kind of guy.

"Mahalo for your stay miss Caceres, your room has been paid for and there's a car out front waiting for you to drive you to Honolulu International." Said the concierge and received a small card from him, it said "I'm waiting." She went out to the car; a black Mercedes was waiting for her. Someone opened the door and there was David.

"Did you pay for my room?" she said, and David got out, he hugged her and said "Yeah, so now you have to ride with me to the airport.

I've got some miles so what you say to upgrade our tickets home with a mildly stop to NY?" She smiled, sat next to him in the car and they went off.

Watching the coastline on their way to Honolulu, he asked the driver to stop for a minute. They had approximately 4 hours to board the plane so there was no rush, both got out of the car and stood by the coastline. David put his arm around her and said "I'm not going to propose, only to make you a promise: If you leave me again, I'm going to lock your hand to mine and never give back the key."

Celia laughed, she took his hand and replied with certainty "I promise to stay locked to your hand, because I realized that there's no one else I'd rather be with. I love you, David." He pulled her closer, kissed her temple and they went back to the car.

The plane from Honolulu International was on time, they were sitting in business class together and enjoyed the view and the decision to have a spontaneous relationship without the formality of getting married. They were devoted to each other, so the marriage thing could wait. At least now, Celia wasn't afraid.

CHAPTER 7:
STARS ALIGHNED

It had been 6 months since Celia and David were back together, he had moved into her flat in London. David's daughter Ally lived with them most of the time, he made an offer to their boss to buy the apartment so he could kick down a wall to make space for Ally's own bedroom.

Everything hadn't been all roses with Ally, she was mad for Celia being gone too long but she understood that grown up problems weren't her problems. So, she forgave her and was now incredibly happy to have a normal popular mom. A mom that could be there for her, be her friend and talk girl talk with.

While cooking dinner, she felt a warm feeling of having her very own family: she didn't need to have her own children to have a child. She had a perfect daughter who trusted her, saw her as the mother she deserved instead of the irresponsible one, was her best friend and was daughter to the man she loved. She moved away from the kitchen to see what they were doing: he was reading a book, with the smaller lamp on and his glasses. Ally was finishing her homework, looked up and saw her looking. She ran over to hug her mom and she carried her in to sit next to her father. "Dinner's ready, shall we eat here with a good movie?" David looked up and those glasses made him look even more delicious than dinner, he came over to the couch where they were now sitting, gave them both a kiss on the forehead and said, "Here should be good, I'll fetch the plates."

They watched a movie while eating, when they were done, Celia took the plates and went to the kitchen to clean up.

David came to the kitchen with the last things, he picked up the clean rag and started to dry the plates. She felt a tear run down her cheek but managed to clear it before he could see her. He put down the rag and put his arms around her, he kept his cheek close to hers "I love how normal we are. No loud nights, people we barely know, just us and the family. This is the only thing we need. I love this, us like this." She smiled and threw some soap on him, he laughed and picked up the rag to throw it on her. Ally came to the rescue; she was laughing so hard at them.

Bedtime for the child, quality time for them. David came with 2 glasses of peach iced tea and sat next to her in the sofa. He put his arm around her and just sat there, while drinking. "You know, we should go to the movies tomorrow. What do you think?" he said. Celia checked the phone to see what movies were on, it had been a while since they went to the cinema. "What do you fancy? Romance, action, child?" she said, and he whispered "With you by my side, anything works. Although there's this new movie with Christian Bale that I really really want to see, do you mind?" She laughed, kissed him on the cheek and said "Are you kidding? I love his movies, hello Batman!"

Celia was walking to the office, first day to the see her boss since she left to work from home in her new home London.

He was waiting in the London based office, which she had never visited since she only worked in the Birmingham one.

Bert was talking to someone on the phone, when he saw her, he waved her in. She sat down in the closest chair, took out some reports that he needed to see. "Hey Celia, so nice to have you back. Well not in the usual spot but you know. How has it been? Everything okay with David?" She smiled and nodded; David was working downstairs in the KBT department. He worked with people who had anxiety issues regarding specific things like all sorts of bugs, animals, certain consistence in food etc.

"You wanted to buy the apartment? David said something about knocking down a wall to build a bedroom for his girl, but there's no need to buy. I'll be happy to give you the apartment, you both have done so much for the company and well I'm incredibly happy to have you professionals on this team. Do what you need, it's all yours." Said Bert and took out 2 glasses, one he filled with some whisky and one with non-alcoholic champagne. "Here's to you, wonderful woman that truly make a difference here. Thank you for staying. Cheers!" Celia smiled, clinked his glass, and had some champagne. It was a bit weird, since she didn't drink normally anything besides iced tea or any juice.

"Thank you, Bert, this means so much for us…especially for Ally, my newly bonus daughter. Well, I should get back to work, I have some reports to write and a prescription for a patient. I'll see you and thank you again." She said and left the office. Went back to hers, funny the door was open. She entered and someone closed it behind her, it was David. "Hey baby, how did it go with the boss? Did he accept my proposal to buy the apartment?" they hugged and kissed, Celia kept him in her arms and told him the good news.

"We can hire someone who can help, this is great! When would you like to start?" said David and was very eager to begin working with the bedroom, Celia went to check her schedule. "Um, I think during the first 2 weeks of July, then I can help you. Who works with this kind of job? You know anyone?" According to David, his friend from back in the day, Alex could help them out. But during that time, they couldn't stay in the apartment because of the plaster dust. So, he suggested that they could travel to Paris for a week, something Ally would be happy about since Disneyland was somewhere she always wanted to visit. Well, so did Celia.

"Ready to go home? It's almost 9 pm, you've been working 2 extra hours. Come on then, off we go." Said David and moved Celia's chair, as she was finishing writing the reports. "Hey hey, I'm almost done, I got to file these tonight otherwise I can't continue tomorrow. I think you're making me stall my work sir, maybe I need to punish you." She said almost laughing, while she hit save and archived the patient files. David turned the chair towards her and said, "You know, now that you're sitting there all comfortable, maybe I could give you a lap dance." His cheeky smile made her blush, he was the only man that could do that to her. She thought about when she was younger, in her teen years when everything went to hell with her former boyfriend after catching him with her friend Rosalyn.

Celia became an emo, a girl who dressed in black or grey, had dark eyeliner and dyed her hair black as well.

She didn't do the piercings or anything like that, but she did get a permanent tattoo on her wrist, now faded. Maybe she could tattoo it permanently this time, it meant a lot to her: a Japanese sign that meant Family. The only people she could count on at that difficult time in her life. Heartbreak is serious in that age, especially for a girl. Then it was that other guy, from the university… Mark. She liked him so much that they first went on a trip (as friends) to Barcelona, she kind of hoped something would happen but nope nothing. He's gay now by the way, maybe somewhere deep down she always knew.

"Miss Caceres, what can I tempt you with today? Maybe some old fashion lap dance or a strip tease?" David said and she came back to today, a 39-year-old woman with a serious boyfriend and daughter. She smiled, if only she could tell her younger self that things get better in time. "Strip tease please but when can do that at home, I can't wait to rip that black shirt of your chest." She said in a low voice, her sexy voice according to David. "Oh darling, you're in for a treat. Come on, let's go home. I got your bag, here's your jacket." He said and pushed her gently through the door, pressed for the elevator and stole kisses from her while they waited.

Finally at home, Ally was with Celia's parents playing with her sister's oldest kid and was going to have a sleepover to give the couple a night off. She didn't mind, she loved Celia's family and they loved her. Celia washed her hands and David did the same in the kitchen, put on some cheesy music and waited for her to sit down, she was already laughing at his choice of music: Usher's Yeah. He began dancing, it was dorky moves, but she loved it.

He moved closer to her and let her remove something, she chose his jacket, and he threw it on the floor. Then it was his socks, the tie which he put on her shoulders, he teased her nose with it and continued, she couldn't hold her laughter anymore. She got up from the sofa and went to dance with him, they laughed together, suddenly it wasn't about stripping anymore but slow dancing. He purred close to her ear, it did sound more like a satisfied mmm, like after dinner. They danced for a while and he said, "I can't get paid now, I'm slow dancing." Celia smiled, she nibbled his earlobe and whispered "I'm paying whether it's slow or fast, you're the best dancer ever. I'm coming back here."

"I have to say, this is beautiful, we can't thank you enough for this amazing job. She's going to be thrilled!" David said shook hands with Alex, the handyman that made the room for Ally. She was at Celia's parents for the time being and now she would come home to her very own room! The walls were in a light pink shade, white furniture and the bed was quite simple with lavender sheets. Celia was admiring his work and squeezed David's hand, he took out his wallet and said "How much did we say? £2500? I'll leave it at 3, you did an amazing job man. My kid is thrilled and so are we. I owe you!"

Alex was very satisfied with his job too, a true artist. His wife was expecting their 2nd child any day now, so any job was welcome. He said his goodbyes and left, while David and Celia decided to make some lunch for them, later they were going to pick up Ally from the parents and surprise her with this masterpiece.

Pasta salad on the balcony, discussing what more they could do for fun during summer besides working. David checked his phone and suggested "Hey, why don't we make Paris a given choice? We all have current passports, no need to get a VISA, here look! Paris, a week in a nice hotel in Montmartre and visit to Disneyland. What do you think?" Celia didn't have any current bookings for the next weeks, so it wasn't a bad idea.

"You know what babe, let's do it! Book it and we'll split it, so it will be fair shared." She said and he frowned but accepted in the end. He knew not to argue with his girlfriend too much.

Ally was thrilled with her new room, although she liked it at Celia's parent's house. She slept in Celia's old room, with some of her memories on the wall: pictures from her convention visits when she was younger, the latest was with Tom Ellis, actor from hit series "Lucifer". Celia had told her that it was a great experience, he was such a nice guy and that she was so nervous that he had to hold on to her so she wouldn't fall. He reminded her of her dad, there was kindness in his eyes. "Momma, you know that picture you have with Tom Ellis in your old bedroom. He kind of reminds me of dad, they have similar eyes. Did you have a crush on him?" Ally had this cheeky smile in her eyes, like she really wanted her to compare. "Yes, I did, your dad though is more like his earlier character Gary. That's who I fell in love with, a calm and quiet guy…your father." David was chuckling in the corner, she told him this years ago and he thought it was hilarious. Of course, by that time they were just friends, and she skipped the love part, something David remembered well.

Because that was when he fell in love with Celia, when she just wanted to be friends was when he felt like there was something missing in his life.

"You know, we should talk about the family trip we're about to do sweetie. We're going to, drumroll please… Disneyland in Paris!" said Celia and tried to divert the conversation. Ally was ecstatic and she wanted all the details about hotel and how close they would be. Her favorites were Toy story and she couldn't wait to meet Buzz Lightyear.

Celia was on the computer late night, finishing some transcripts for her latest patient visit. It was almost midnight, and she was getting tired, she checked her memory storage where she found old pictures from the conventions she assisted: London in 2019, London 2018, Birmingham 2017, and Barcelona 2012. She was happy, younger, and well it was good times. Now she was an adult, well in some ways and incredibly happy to be in such a good relationship with both her boyfriend and his daughter. She grew up in a good home but her step-father didn't exactly roll out the welcome wagon when she really needed a father, but he wasn't always like that.

When she was little, he adored her, but people tend to change. After her summer camp, she felt like an outsider in her own family, and it was very painful. That's when she found out that he wasn't her real father, not from himself but from his friend.

It was blurted out by mistake and Celia became an introvert: she didn't want to play with the others and was mostly by herself. That's the biggest reason why she stayed alone for so long time, she had serious trust issues and had to see a therapist for 6 years.

Her stepfather taught her that men cheat, it's in their nature and that they only wanted women for sex. So yeah, she couldn't possibly trust a guy asking her out when she was a teenager nor later as an adult. Celia kept in mind what he said, also when she caught him cheating on her mom during a visit to the mall with a classmate. That's when she had an accident and suffered partial memory loss. She was in a hospital for 3 months and when she came back, her stepfather took off. Years later she recovered almost completely and understood why he left, something that always haunted her because she missed some pieces in her giant puzzle called life.

She was teary again; it was like pain was constantly living in her heart. David was watching her from the kitchen door, ran over quietly and put his arms around her "Hey, hey, what's going on? I thought you were happy about Paris?" She moved closer to him, felt some of his perfume on his shirt and sniffed "I am, I just found some old pictures of my conventions and it got me into thinking back to when I was a kid. My stepdad and all that, you know. It just came back, the pain and suffering that he caused." She sighed and David got down on his knees, held her face with both hands and said "Listen, he hurt you and your family, but he can't anymore. He's long gone and he'll never come back, trust me he's ashamed. If not, he should and you shouldn't waste your tears on him. Your family loves you and we love you, he doesn't matter anymore. Come on, I'll do a special lap dance for you, no charge." He gave her a cheeky smile and took his hand.

In their bedroom, he sat her down, removed his shirt and her blouse. No music since Ally was asleep but she could hear calm piano music in her head, it was the soundtrack to the "Lucifer" series. David wasn't dancing, just removing his clothes slowly. When he was in his boxers she stood up and sat him down, she kissed him passionately as they fell onto the bed. His hands caressed her back, it was never creepy to be touched by him. She noticed the small freckles below his eyes and on his nose, he was so beautiful, her future husband. She touched his nose and he nuzzled into her hand, he kissed her with need, he whispered in her ear that he loved her, and she took a deep breath. They made sweet love that night, before falling asleep in each other's arms.

CHAPTER 8:
PARIS

Bienvenu a Charles de Gaulle, Paris" said the plane voice before they touched down in their biggest airport. Ally had just woken up; Celia was holding her head and David held her hand. They waited until most of the people got off before getting ready to get off the plane. Paris was beautiful and crowded, at least airport wise. They got their bags and took the airport coach to Gare du Nord, their train station and meeting point. From there it was a walk to Montmartre and the hotel Timhotel.

"At last, a shower and maybe some food, you girls hungry?" said David and checked that the bathroom was in order. The whole suit was beautiful, with a view over Sacre Coeur. Ally got a big bed close to the window all to herself and the parents the bigger bed in the center. "Well, I guess we'll just skip the lovemaking until we get home, huh babe?" David whispered in Celia's ear while she unloaded the clothes into the closets. She pinched him carefully and he stole a kiss, luckily Ally didn't hear anything, she was too busy checking out the room.

Celia took a shower first, then David because Ally didn't need one. Changing of clothes and then out the door to discover beautiful Paris. The sun was shining but not too hot, perfect this time of the year. They took some photos, family photos and crazy ones. It was their first vacation as a family, otherwise Ally had never been abroad with her dad. Her mother wasn't in the mood for travelling when they were a couple so within the UK mostly otherwise Birmingham.

They had lunch in a restaurant nearby before continuing to Notre Dame, still in reconstruction after the massive fire a few years ago.

"From this cathedral came the story of Quasimodo, the one from Disney but originally written by Victor Hugo, a French writer." Celia told Ally and she was mesmerized by the massive church. "Momma, do you think he lives there?" she pointed towards the belltower, where most of the gargoyles sat. "I'm sure he does honey, whenever they ring the bells, it's Quasi that does that." She explained and David wrinkled his nose in happiness. Celia was a special woman; she told the best history lessons in a form that children could understand. She should've been a teacher.

"Momma, the fire that happened here…do you think Frodo did this?" Ally said, looking a bit worried. She nodded and told her it had been an electrical fault, that the church had new installations and that probably caused the fire.

They continued through the streets of Paris until they reached Sacre Coeur and then back to the hotel, Ally needed a shower and whiles she was there, the parents could have some alone time. Celia was lying on the couch on David's lap, almost falling asleep while he caressed her face. "Ally was impressed by your story telling babe, why didn't you become a teacher? You're a skilled therapist but still, you should consider. Many kids would love to hear you." He said and bent down to kiss her, she smiled. "I like teaching, but I don't know, I have a friend who's a teacher and the kids, are so disrespectful. Well, the take after their parents as well."

David pulled her up from his legs to kiss her more, this was becoming a little more intense than before.

She stopped him calmly "Hey, remember that Ally's in the bathroom. Maybe we can save this for tonight? The bathroom is comfy, we can try there?" He purred in their kiss "Mm I don't if I can wait that long, but yeah…she could be shocked otherwise. I'll be calm, but I can't promise anything." Celia smiled "Well you'll have to, here she comes. Hey sweetie, how was the bath?" Ally was drying her hair with the towel, but she could barely keep her eyes open "I'm so tired, just want to sleep but my hair…" David went to get the hairdryer and they both helped her dry it so she could sleep.

"I think she's asleep, wait 15 minutes and come to the bathroom." Celia said and went in, closed the door with lock. In there she changed into some lingerie she had bought before the trip that David had not seen: a black lace nightgown. It must have been less than 15 minutes when he knocked quietly on the door, she let him in and he said, "Alright then, where were we?" He almost tripped when he saw Celia, she looked so gorgeous, and he just shut the door before wrapping his arms around her waist. They kissed intensely; he had moved her against the wall right by the door in case Ally woke up. She removed his t-shirt and kissed his neck while he tried to lift her gown, his breath felt hot on her cold skin and when he finally got inside her, they moved to the floor carefully.

"Wow, that was, wow." He said, while lying right next to her. She smiled and sat up, he got up to kiss her again. They were wrapped up in each other's arms, comfortable on the bathroom floor. "You know, maybe we should get some sleep. It's almost 11 pm and tomorrow we're going to Disneyland, come on…brush your teeth." Celia said and helped him up, he grabbed her waist and looked at the mirror. Their eyes met and both smiled "I love you silly." She said and turned over to kiss him, he responded and handed over her toothbrush.

The following morning, they got ready for their big day in Disneyland. First up breakfast in the hotel restaurant and then a quick walk to Gare du Nord. From there another short stop before reaching the gates of the magical world. Ally was hyped, she was so well rested after the long walks in Paris the day before.

Not many people by the entrance, it was still early in the morning. Someone in line said something that it becomes crazy after noon, so maybe they should eat lunch before all want. They went to Sleeping Beauty's castle, a few rides and Ally met her hero: Buzz Lightyear. She was so happy to hug him and a lot of pictures later they continued their journey.

It was now 8 pm and it was time to go back to the hotel, they were all tired and sweaty. They took turns to shower; Celia adjusted the thermostat to cool down the room and they went to sleep. It had been a long day but she couldn't rest entirely, she got out of bed carefully not to wake David and went to the reception "Good evening, do you have a computer I could borrow? I'm having some problems with my Wi-Fi connection."

The night guard showed her a computer in a corner by the front desk, she thanked him and checked her emails and if there was anything that needed to be assisted. No news, so everything was working simply fine back home.

She thanked him again and went back to her room, David was up, coming from the bathroom and realized that she wasn't asleep "Hey, where did you go? Everything okay?" Celia smiled and nodded, she gave him a kiss and went to the bathroom to change clothes, he followed her to watch her change. Suddenly his desire look awoke her lust as well, they shut the door quietly and this time she stripped for him. It would seem like their time apart only made them stronger as a couple, lately having time for themselves weren't just to sleep together but also go on dates and have quality time: cook dinner, bake, or dance.

He was sitting on chair by the wall, while she stripped out of her home clothes. Normal guys wouldn't find it attractive to see their girlfriends in sweatpants and t-shirt but for David it was more the way she was.

Celia was approximately 5,3, a bit Rubenesque with dark red hair, kind eyes and always a big smile. He admired her; she had come a long way since the shy girl he met so many years ago. She was always focused on work and left everything else on the side, it wasn't the first time he was admiring her from afar wondering what life together would be like.

While standing still in her sweatpants, braless and beautiful he stood up and grabbed her shoulders to kiss her.

His lips moved to her neck, down her collarbone, the middle of her chest down to her belly. He removed her pants carefully, sat down and sat her on top of him. They moved in sync, in their kiss, moaning into each other's mouths. Celia gasped when they reached climax and pressed her nose to his mouth, he kissed it, holding her in his arms for a while. "I was worried when you weren't there, for a moment I thought you had left but your suitcase was still in the closet so I figured you might have gone for a walk. Did something happen?" he said and held her hand while she climbed of him. "No, I just had some problems with the Wi fi connection and went downstairs to borrow the computer. No emails, nothing so I came back. I did tell Bert about our vacation, but you know, people always tend to write an email or so. I guess I can relax completely now. And no, I'm never leaving you again baby. I'm not afraid." David grabbed her waist and she giggled, he held her in his arms, and she felt something wet falling on her bare shoulders, he was crying.

"No no, why are you crying? I just said that I'll never leave again. Baby, hey, hey come on now. Sit down for a minute." She said and sat him down on the chair again, he sniffled, and he looked like a teenager that just had his heart broken for the first time. Celia sat in his lap for a while, just held each other for some time. Hopefully, they wouldn't wake Ally from her sleep. "Celia, I'm such a fool. That year when I decided to leave, I wanted to turn in the door and come back, kiss you like never but I just froze. I know I wasted 4 years but never again, I'll never let you go. I love you more than my own life, if you left again, I would die of sadness. Please, promise me that you'll never leave."

He sniffled in her hair, she turned her face towards him and said "Never again, I promise. Now, what do you say to another go? I'm up for it." He couldn't say no to her.

"Ally, did you pack your things? Stuffed animal? The candy? No, you can put it here. We'll check the bag, you can carry your bag only baby. David, did we forget anything?" said Celia and counted the bags, David was going through the closets, but nothing left behind. "Nope all clear, I think we have everything. Shall we?" he said and opened the door, Ally rang the elevator button, and they closed the door behind them. It was time to go back to London, a sunny Saturday morning from the city of love to the city of fog.

The ride to the airport was calm, Ally slept, David and Celia shared funny looks at each other. At Charles de Gaulle, they checked in their bags and went through security, approached the gate but still had 2 hours more to go before boarding so they had lunch at Chez Remi. It was time for the boarding, unfortunately coach was over-booked but they offered first class which they happily took. The most comfortable journey home, to a sunny London, no fog this time.

At London Heathrow, mom and dad were waiting for their arrival. Hugs and kisses at baggage claim, Ally was too busy telling them about her meeting with Buzz Lightyear. David and Celia walked hand in hand, though he carried the carrier with all their bags to the car. Celia's dad drove, Ally rode shotgun and the other three sat in the back.

It didn't get better when David was trying to grope Celia during the ride home. Her parents had been watching the apartment while they were away and would leave the next day to Birmingham, but David had a different opinion "say Mr. and Mrs. Caceres, would you mind staying a little longer in London let's say until next weekend to watch Ally? I wanted to take out my girl for some alone time if you don't mind." Celia's dad looked into the mirror to meet David's eyes but when he looked at Ally, she was looking hopeful that they could stay. "Sure son, no problem."

They got home to their flat, left the dirty clothes in the bathroom baskets and then exchanged for the clean ones. David whispered in Celia's ear "Don't bring too many clothes, we're not leaving the hotel." His winking eyes confirmed her suspicion, he wanted a week of sex basically. Although it wasn't just like that, he was very tender to her. They said goodbye to parents and daughter, he grabbed the car keys and loaded their bags. "Where are we going?" Celia finally said, he looked cheeky at her but told her nothing. She sighed; London was a city filled with surprises so it could be anywhere in the area.

CHAPTER 9:
PROPOSALS IN PLURAL

The car stopped by the Thistle in central London, it was close by the area where she used to stay although never this fancy. The room was very standard but had AC by the entrance, something Celia always searched for. She turned it on and watched David put the bags in the closet, they exchanged smiles as he moved closer to her. He gave her a hug, sniffed her neck, and held her tight. He proceeded to kiss her forehead, her eyelids, her nose, her cheeks and finished on her lips.

He tasted like chocolate, she smiled because she did see him take one of the complementary mints on the pillow. "Did you eat the chocolate?" she said during their kiss, he laughed and pulled her closer. "Yeah, I did. Couldn't help myself, hey, um, do you want to move this interesting conversation to the bed maybe?" He purred in her ear, lead her to the big bed, sat down and pulled her down onto him. They laughed, he was very handsy, touching her thighs gently. Celia was happy, she laughed when he tickled her and finally rested her head on his chest. They were still fully dressed, but it felt nice to just be there.

David stroke her back, helped her up from her waist before sitting up. "It's almost 5 pm, maybe we should have dinner. Want to go out or order in? Maybe the menu is good here." Celia let him kiss her collarbone, let out a mmm before saying "Let's go to M&S, they have a great menu and the best lemon cakes."

They went out, hand in hand towards the subway to Bond Street, from there walked to M&S at the end of the street.

It wasn't crowded even though it was late afternoon, Celia made a short stop at the clothes department to buy something to Ally but David told her that they could do it after dinner. The couple found a table by the window and placed their orders for different Chinese dishes and two different cakes for dessert.

David was exquisite in his white shirt with black sweater, his aftershave was subtle, but Celia thought that his natural smell made the aftershave even more seductive. They ate in almost silence but suddenly David pulled out a small box, the well-known Tiffany box.

"I hope I'm not putting off your appetite or scare you off but I want to marry you one day. It doesn't have to be now or within this year, but at some point. I would love it if you would consider wearing my name but if you don't want to it's okay, just marry me, Celia. Be my wife, please." He had glittering eyes, funny how some men are incredibly sensitive and others wouldn't care less. She sighed, but this time it wouldn't feel like she was making a mistake, Celia genuinely loved him, and she also knew that a life together was all she ever wanted.

"No David, now it's my turn. I want you to marry me, it was a mistake to let you go last time and I never thought that you would come back. For a moment I thought, I'll never love anyone again but the truth is that I never loved anyone until I met you. So now I'm asking... David James Castle, will you do me the honor of being my husband, forever and always?" she surprised him with a small black box, inside a white gold band with her name inside. No date since they needed to make it official soon enough.

A tear came down his cheek and he said, "Yes Celia, I'll marry you!" They hugged, a few people in the restaurant applauded and the chef came out with this piece of cake that said "Yes". She put the ring on his finger, and he took out the one from Tiffany's an put it on hers. They kissed and continued their meals, before talking a walk-through Hyde Park and ending the night back at Thistle.

"I'll get you a new one when we get married, this one is for engagement only." He said while he was brushing his teeth, Celia was changing clothes into her lingerie, another set he hadn't seen. She was extremely nervous, tonight she was an engaged woman and would spend the night with her engaged fiancée. She could see him in his black pajama pants and no shirt, something she insisted on because he was so handsome in bare chest. He had these freckles from his shoulders and he didn't have that really fit body, but he was so gorgeous that to her he was perfect.

She sat on the bed, with a bunch of pillows and tried her best to look seductive. David had still not seen her and was just turning of the light when he finally looked. He stood there with semi open mouth and said, "Excuse me miss, I am an engaged man." He walked towards the bed, took away the pillow and threw it on the floor, sat down next to her and whispered, "I don't know what you're doing to me but I surely don't want you to stop, you smell great." Celia chuckled, moved closer to him and he let the tiny strap of her lingerie slip down her shoulder leaving it bare. He kissed her shoulder, and she closed her eyes, just enjoying the moment.

She was now sitting with her back towards him, while he carefully removed the other strap and let it fall down her other shoulder. He wrapped his arms around her, and she held him with her hands, he turned her over to face him but got up on her knees, so her chemise slowly fell onto the bed.

David smiled, it wasn't just lust in his eyes but pure love. He moved onto the closest pillow and moved Celia towards it, then caressed her from face to belly. She felt an electricity bolt pass through her and moved her hand towards his face, he kissed it and moved closer to her face. They were staring into each other's eyes, nose to nose and breathing in each other. "You know, I've never felt like this with anyone. You can take my breath away with so little as a smile or with a kiss, I am at your mercy."

Celia smiled, in David's mind she was like a young girl: shy and sensitive but with the mind of a strong woman: seductive and unafraid. He held out his hand and she put hers towards his, slightly smaller than him but in sync they matched. His sigh was what made her throw herself on him and they kissed fiercely, David moved his hands to her waist, and she tried to remove his pants.

He was ecstatic, she was exceptionally good at seducing him and now he could barely breathe. "Okay I think we need to catch our breaths for a while, want me to order some chocolate?"

She was lying by his side, hiding in his chest when she nodded a yes to the chocolate but before it arrived, she was already asleep in his arms. He called back to the room service to leave it outside the door, his girl needed to sleep a little.

CHAPTER 10:
ENGAGEMENT PARTY PLANS

You're engaged?! OMG! Congratulations!! When is the wedding?" said Celia's mom when she showed her the ring. She smiled "I don't know yet mom, we just got back. I'm unsure to have a big wedding though, I think city hall should be good. When I know more, I'll let you know. Where's Ally?"

"She's in her room, are you going to tell her?" Celia's mom said, and she was already entering the girl's room. "Hey honey, we're back. How have you been?" she said and gave her a hug, Ally was so happy to see her again.

"I missed you momma, it was fun with grandparents though, but you know, I love you most!" the girl said and hugged her even tighter. Celia sat down with Ally on her bed and said "You know honey, I love you too. And your daddy, so we decided something while we were away. We're getting married and I want you to be my flower girl, okay?" David's daughter was thrilled; she threw herself onto Celia and she was already crying because she had something else in mind too. "Not only will you be my flower girl, but I officially want to ask you, if you'll do me the honor of being my daughter. You'll have your daddy's last name and mine if you want. I can never replace your mom but I'll do my best to be the one you need."

Ally was crying too "Yes mommy, I want you to be my mommy. And I'm happy to be your daughter and that you are marrying daddy.

Does he know?" she asked, and David was standing in the doorway, Celia nodded, and he hugged all three.

Celia was in the laundry room, loading the final batch of dirty clothes into the washer machine, Ally was asleep in her room and David was doing the dishes. It was a normal afternoon in the future Castle/Caceres house, when the cell rang. It wasn't Celia's, hers was on the table in the kitchen with music on. It was David's "Yeah? Hey Tamara, no it's good. No sorry, she's asleep, yeah well, she takes naps on weekends. I'll tell her to call you when she wakes up. Fine, yeah, I'll tell her. Yup, bye." He threw the phone on the table by the microwave and continued with the dishes, Celia came out and put her arms around his waist. "Hey, you…was that?" she began, and David tilted his head around, gave her a kiss, saying "Yeah, Tamara. She wanted to talk to Ally but I told her she's asleep, don't really know why she calls." She could tell that Tamara, who hadn't call in an awfully long time still managed to make him angry.

"Babe, hang on a sec. Maybe Tamara turned her life around, she has a right you know to see her daughter. Maybe we shouldn't deny her the possibility to see her or even talk to her." Celia said and kissed his shoulder, David sighed heavily.

"She should've thought about it before letting her go just like that, I'll talk to Ally but I don't think she would want to. Besides, I have no interest in seeing Tamara again. That woman ruined my life."

Celia sat down by the kitchen table and said "If you want and if she wants, I'll bring Ally to see her. I don't mind, she made mistakes yes but she's her biological mother. And you both made the girl, and she's perfect." David looked at her, at first, he had this frown look on his face but then when he understood her point, he went over with his soapy hands to kiss her. "You're a wonderful person, see the light everywhere. If you're sure, then yes please, take Ally to see her mother. Thank you, for being my light."

She smiled and began going through the fridge to see what dinner they should make that evening.

Celia and Ally were on the train to see her mother back in Birmingham. It was their first trip on their own, David was working, and Celia took some time off to be with her daughter. They would also see her parents and sister for a short moment, because her mother wanted to go over some of the engagement preparations. For a moment Celia thought, it would've been better to elope but she knew how important it was for David too.

At Birmingham Central they got off and walked towards their subway station. Ally's mother lived close to Millennium Point; she was going to meet them in the nearby park.

Celia saw a woman with dark hair sitting by a bench in Birmingham Science Garden. Ally held her hand and squeezed it "Mom, I think it's her right there." They went closer, the woman was holding a stuffed animal and suddenly she saw Ally. She gave her a weak smile and got up, Ally wouldn't let go of Celia's hand but approached the woman to greet her. "Oh sweetie, it's been so long. How are you?"

Ally talked to her for a while, accepted the stuffed animal and kept looking at Celia that was sitting underneath a tree in the shadows to give them some space. She smiled when their eyes met, and Ally was calm again. Suddenly both were standing in front of her, and the visit was over, Tamara shook her hand and said goodbye to Ally. "I hope you can come and see me again soon, thank you Celia for taking your time to bring her here. Send my regards to David, and I'm sorry for all the trouble I've made." Celia nodded kindly and took Ally's hand, they left to her mother's house.

They were incredibly happy to see them again, while Grandpa Fred was playing chess with Ally, Celia's mom was showing her some wedding dresses. "This one is a classic, you'll look so beautiful in this dear. Eggshell is a perfect color, I don't know if you want a veil though." She smiled but said "Uh mom, I'm not wearing eggshell. I can't marry in white if I'm not a virgin, besides, you know me. I want a lavender dress, below the knees and flat black ballerinas oh and a small veil like this one should do the trick." Celia showed her mom her phone, there was the perfect dress with attires accordingly.

It was something that could fit her and maybe wear again at some point in life besides, she was even more happy to know that her eldest daughter was getting married.

Back home in London, the girls were both tired and exhausted after their journey. Ally went straight to the shower and Celia was checking the mail, David had not come home yet. It was almost 6 pm and they were having dinner in front of the tv, still nothing from him. She sent a text "Hey honey, we're home and made some potato salad to go with a nice steak. Hope you'll be home soon, we miss you. Love you, bye."

It was now 9 pm, Ally was already asleep in her bed and Celia was worried that no news from David had arrived in all day. She tried calling him, but it went straight to voicemail, she didn't leave messages and went to the bathroom to check on some clothes. Suddenly she heard the door, there he was, with some big packages in hand. "Hey, you, okay?" she said tiredly, and David gave her a little smile. "Hey baby, how was the trip? Will you give me a hand with this?"

She took the packages and put them by the entrance, it was November so it could be Christmas presents. "Sorry that I didn't call, I've been busy all day and when I saw your text, I was already on my way home. How was it? Did Ally like her?" he said, while washing his hands.

"Yeah, they talked, she was happy to see her again. She's changed, you know. Even asked if we could visit again oh and she apologizes to you for everything."

David looked surprised, it wasn't like Tamara to apologize for anything, not even for something so important as to not wanting to raise their daughter. "Well, thank you and I'm not sure how to respond to that. Anyway, come and look what I bought to us." He was eager to show Celia what he bought: a brand-new stereo to Ally, a blu ray player to the living room and some kitchen attires. "Wow, it's beautiful honey but it wasn't necessary. We can manage with what we have, why don't you tell me what is really going on?" They sat down on the sofa,

David was very weird in his behavior but finally came clean "I know we said that we could wait with the wedding, but I booked a venue, I'm sorry but I really really like this place and I know you will too. It's at S:t Paul's cathedral and in 3 weeks from now."

Celia was relieved that it wasn't something worse, like he might be cheating or so. She gave him weak smile and let out a little laughter "Is that why you were so weird? I thought you were going to tell me you were cheating or something, God! Wow, S:t Paul's. You know, I been in the yard but never inside, but I thought you didn't want to get married in a church. What changed your mind?" she asked and took his hand; he was squeezing it but calmed down. "I passed by one day, back when you left.

I imagined us going out through that door and I think I sat down for a while, this priest talked to me, and we became friends. I saw him the other day, he asked how everything was going and I told him that you finally said yes. So, he offered, as a wedding gift to marry us here when we choose. And why I chose in 3 weeks was because in that time, it would be exactly 10 years since we first met. I know it's dorky and I totally get why you left in the first place."

He was looking down at his and her hands when she placed her other hand on his sad cheek, he tilted his face to kiss her and she responded "Then under those terms, I do. I'll marry you in 3 weeks from now at S:t Paul's. That was a beautiful reason and a great gift, but you're a great man. I love you." They hugged and just sat there, happy.

CHAPTER 11:
WEDDING JITTERS

I don't like the model mom, I told you, something classic. I'm not looking like a giant marshmallow!!" Celia said from the dressing room at Debenhams. It was the 4th dress she was trying, none of her own choice. She had told her mother what kind of dress she wanted but her mother insisted on trying something in eggshell white. When she was ready to leave, her mother knocked on the door and said, "I think this one is more you." She slipped in a lavender dress, simple design and just below the knee. With them came a pair of lavender Vans and this little white veil, funny enough called birdcage. Celia took the items and tried everything on, even she felt perfect and had to sit down to calm herself.

"Can I see?" said her mom and opened the door when Celia quietly whispered "Yes". She looked so beautiful; it was just how she had imagined only something was missing. "I think this is your missing item, Grandpa's necklace. I know he wanted you to use it on your special day and how much he wanted to give you away, but Fred wants to do the honor, if you accept." The necklace in silver with the cross and the medallion of Saint Teresa matched perfectly to Celia's slightly pale skin. She never liked golden colors; the reason David had bought a white gold engagement ring.

"I'll be happy to have daddio Fred accompany me mom, you know I love him like my own father. I got to tell you though, I'm freaking out!" she said and sat down in the changing room.

Her mother stroked her head and said "David is a good man; he has made you happier than any other before and you know he genuinely loves you. You know that you've got nothing to be afraid of. You'll be the best of wives and the happiest. Trust in God."

"It's wedding jitters, perfectly normal at this stage. Young woman is marrying and wonders if the guy is the one, trust me if he wasn't the one for you even I would tell you call off the wedding." Said Fred and laughed from the kitchen, Celia was in the living room in their home in Birmingham. She was on weekend visit while David and Ally had a special father-daughter weekend on their own in town, but also because they were going through a special surprise for Celia for the wedding.

His grandmother in Birmingham had left him a beautiful heirloom: a bracelet, but since the silver was getting rusty, he visited a jeweler to change it to white gold. Apart from that, he needed to fill out the papers to change Ally's last names. The phone suddenly rang, David didn't recognize the number "Castle, yeah. Yes, I know her, did something happen? What? I'm her ex, we have a daughter in common. Oh, God, yeah, I'll be right there. Thank you, bye."

Tamara was in the hospital, critical condition. Apparently, she tried to commit suicide and they neighbor called it in. He called Celia "Hey baby, I need you to come to the Birmingham City hospital as soon as possible. Ally's mother Tamara, she tried to kill herself.

Yeah, she's at City but I don't know how long, yeah, she's with me but I'll stop by Alex's house and tell them to watch her. How soon? I'll meet you there. Love you too, bye."

David got to the hospital much faster than Celia, asked at the reception where he could find Tamara. She was in a little room with tubes in her throat and on life support, no reaction when he spoke to her. He sat down and pat her hand slowly, he hadn't been close to her since Ally was approximately 4 months old. The doctors told him that she didn't have much time left.

Celia finally arrived, she asked the nurse on call in which room Tamara was and got to the same room where David was. She stopped at the door, without telling him she was right there. Silently she listened to him talk to her, about what he felt when Tamara told him that she was pregnant, when Ally was born and how lonely he felt after their split. Then he spoke out words that Celia wasn't ready to hear "*I love you Tamara*, it hurt me so much when you left and now you're doing it again. *Think of our daughter*, she's going to grow up without you. Come back."

She pressed herself against the doorway to prevent herself from fainting: He still loved her. Tears fell down her cheeks and she couldn't take it anymore. Celia backed away slowly and hid in the bathroom, while trying to grasp what David had just said to his ex-girlfriend Tamara.

She dried her tears, washed her face before opening the door. On her way out, she saw David speaking to the doctor but he didn't see her. Celia turned around a few times, to pretend to be just arriving. She found David's eyes and he looked happy when he saw her, came over to give her a hug in greeting. "Hey, sorry to drag you out here but Tamara tried to kill herself. The doctor said it's just a scare and she'll be okay soon."

She looked at him with sad eyes, maybe this was the jitters she was feeling: this was their end. David looked worried and asked "Are you okay? You look pale, did you eat something?" Celia nodded, she wasn't hungry nor preoccupied for her own health.

"I'm fine, it's great that Tamara is doing better. Is Ally coming?" she said and pretended everything was simply fine. "No, I left her at Alex's. She doesn't need to see her mom like this." He said and immediately regretted saying it like that "I'm sorry, I'm just really worried right now. She's never been like this before and I feel really sorry for her, she doesn't have any family here but Ally and me." Celia took a deep breath, felt some anger in her heart but knew that the best she could do was to call off everything. Tamara needed David and Ally, the only person in the way was Celia herself but she knew if she could just stay away, everything would work out alright.

"David, I need to tell you something. I heard you, from the doorway.

How you spoke to Tamara, how much you still love her and because she's the mother of your child. Maybe it's time for you to have a second chance, to be a family. I don't mind, in fact I'm not even angry at you. I know how hard it is to lose one's family because of other people, don't let it happen to you and Ally." Her voice was cracking, she knew she wouldn't be able to keep talking. Instead, she smiled, weakly and left. He didn't come after her, he didn't call her and he didn't come back to the flat that night.

Those wedding jitters was more like a jittering goodbye.

Celia's phone rang, it was Ally. It had been about a week since she last saw her, right before she went to Birmingham and right before David confessed undying love for his ex-girlfriend Tamara. She took a deep breath and answered, "Hey Ally, how it is going?" but it wasn't her voice on the other end: "Hi Celia, how are you?"

She sighed, didn't really know what to say when pretty much everything was said and done. Right now, she was staying in a hotel nearby, working from her computer rather than going back to the office. Bert, as always very understanding. He offered to pay for the hotel, while he was going through his contacts in case anyone had a flat, he could buy.

"Hi David, I'm fine and you? How's Tamara? And Ally?" she kept pinching her hands to prevent herself from crying out in pain.

David sighed over the phone, he didn't really know what to say. How could he explain to Celia what she had witnessed?

"Celi, I'm so sorry for all this. I've been an idiot, this was not the way it sounded like. Listen, Tamara was in a bad shape, and she needed to hear that someone cares. That's all I do, I care for her. She knows that the only love

I have for her is for Ally, she's our common link. Please, just come home, okay? I know we can work this out."

Celia let her tears run down her cheeks, sure it sounded like it was just that: a man who was confused in his choice of words, someone who wanted to give hope to a dying woman but still, a man can't confess love to someone he doesn't love just like that. It had to be more. She sniffed quietly and said "I'm staying here for the time being, I need to think. So should you, think things over and see what you genuinely want. I've asked Bert for a transfer, I think we should stay apart from now on and it shouldn't affect our jobs. You can keep the flat, see it as a gift from me to Ally. Take care David, give Ally my love and Tamara my best for her recovery. Bye."

She hung up and ran to the bathroom, turned on the tap-water on cold and sunk her face into the sink. Whenever she suffered panic attacks, she took deep breaths of cold steam from the water, she felt her heart break and fainted on the bathroom floor.

CHAPTER 12:
SAY YOU WON'T LET GO

This is a newly renovated apartment with view to the Thames, big windows as you can see, a bathroom with toilet included, a single toilet, closets, big bedroom, an attic that you have sole access to and a parking space. The monthly rent is £350, and it includes internet, electricity, and water. We need a 3-month deposit, and you can have the keys within the week."

The woman from the real estate firm was friends with Bert, she got him a good deal for an apartment close to everything and away from David. For the moment, her few things from the flat in Shepherds Bush were in storage until she could find a place to stay. He didn't make more attempts to talk to her again, so she guessed that he understood what was more important.

Celia paid the rent like the woman said and was able to move in right away. Once again, she was standing in the middle of an empty apartment thinking what had gone wrong.

She placed her computer in the kitchen and connected her little Bluetooth amp to have some music while she cleaned up. First song that came up was a sad one by James Arthur, with a heavy heart she vacuumed, and some tears were shed across the floor.

In another part of town, David was making dinner to him and Ally while Tamara was asleep in the bedroom. She was staying with them now, in Celia's old flat in

Shepherds Bush so she could have company since she didn't have any immediate family nearby.

She was enjoying the perks of having a family now, even though it had been a little bit of an extreme to go that far as attempted suicide. David was caring for her and Ally was growing more attached to her mother, even though she kept Celia close to her heart. She had sent a few messages that she responded but asked nothing if she and her father would get back together.

David was trying to move on, he knew that his mistake cost him his relationship and he wanted Celia back but somehow, he couldn't manage to do something else apart from that phone call that one time from Ally's phone.

Tamara got out of bed after the smell of newly made food and joined them at dinner. It looked like she wasn't in such a bad shape anymore, she was rosy and had a good appetite: "This is so good David, where did you learn to be such a good cook?" He gave her a bothered smile and said something about checking in some of Celia's books, he could tell that Tamara didn't like talking about her more than needed.

"So, um, how is she? Did you talk anymore after my accident?" she said, wiping her mouth. David looked at her with a tired look, he didn't want to discuss his life with her. "No, we haven't. How long did the doctor say you needed supervision?" he said sourly, something she didn't appreciate.

"I'll be with bed rest for at least 4 months but if you want, I can just go back to Birmingham. I'm sure they can help me at the clinic, maybe even send a nurse to keep tabs on me." David sighed, finished part of his meal, and threw the rest in the bin.

"Mom, no one is throwing you out. But dad and Celia aren't talking right now, I don't know if it has something to do with you or not but we're here to help you get back on your feet. She wants you to get better." said Ally and pat on Tamara's hand, who squeezed her hand back.

"I know honey, but since Celia is so kind maybe she can let your father and me be so we can get back together. You know, I've never stopped loving him all this time. Don't you want to see us together?" she said and blinked to David. He did not turn back to watch them nor respond; it would seem like Tamara was back into her old ways: manipulative as always.

In bed he looked at pictures of Celia and him when they were a family. He missed her so much, but he also understood that he blew his chances with her and this time it was for good.

Meanwhile Celia was putting some boxes in her attic storage when she received a text from Bert, her boss: "Hey, it's me. I have some news and I think you're in need of them. The office in New York is available and it's yours if you want it. There's a flat waiting for you close to Central Park and the only thing you need is to bring your stuff to this firm (see attached nr) and they'll expedite them for you. Your salary is according to American laws, by the end of the month and something extra to get you started. The tickets will arrive tomorrow by FedEx. Let me know when you get there, stay safe! /B"

She smiled, this was a great opportunity for her and for her career. It would also mean that David would have a chance to develop his relationship to Tamara and their child, without having her in the way.

Celia dragged her suitcases through the airport to check in for American Airlines 725 to New York, she was about 2 hours early. Long line to check in but then she saw an empty automatic check in line and went over. 2 suitcases and one handbag, she kept the handbag and striped the others with her information: "See you in New York!" she thought to herself before leaving the bags.

"Welcome to Heathrow, we will proceed boarding for American Airlines flight 725 to Newark, New York in Gate 40. Please proceed to show passport and your ticket, we have some free seats in first class to rows 15-20 since we have overbooked in coach. Rows 15-20 please take seats in first class, thank you."

"This is it, goodbye UK and hello US." Celia thought to herself as she entered the plane, to first class by the window.

A very comfy seat, but it also reminded her of her flight home from Hawaii. "Goodbye David." A tear escaped her eye.

CHAPTER 13:
NEW YORK, NEW YORK

Celia had begun her life in New York 12 months ago as chief therapist at the "Live Well" clinic. She loved to live in the city that never sleeps, although her mom wasn't at all amused. She didn't tell them she was leaving because of all the questions about her failed relationship with David, but mostly because it was too far.

Lately they Skyped once a week, sometimes twice. Claire's kids were getting big, and mom and dad were doing simply fine. Ally had stopped by the other day when Claire was walking home from the park. She had asked about Celia but Claire didn't say a word about New York. Just that she had a lot of work and was travelling between the London and Birmingham offices.

Celia didn't have much of a social life, she always began at 9:30 and left around 7 pm. Besides the patients and the cleaners, she didn't meet other people. She barely saw her neighbors and it didn't really matter, lately it was almost like she was avoiding people.

Bert called to check in occasionally, asked if she needed something or maybe even some help but being the workaholic, she declined. He had spoken to David, he asked about her, but Bert only said that she had a lot of work and was travelling between the offices. He didn't want to tell him about her being in New York so instead he said that she was looking to transfer to Tokyo.

Since Bert had a lot of friends, he could probably find something for her there. David had then told him that grownups don't run away and that was when Bert lost it, this time being the first to even address their relationship.

He told him off, that Celia was no coward and that he should've resolved his issues with his ex before proposing to someone else.

"I did resolve them, a long time ago and I told Celia this! It was a mistake to say to Tamara that I loved her because I don't, I never did, not like Celia. Her I love because she changed my life! Bert, please, where is she? Her phone is disconnected so I guess she changed number, you're the only one who can reach her." He didn't want to break, but he felt sorry for the poor sap. So, he told him that she had transferred to the office in the US but that she didn't want to be in contact with David anymore.

"You hurt her badly David, I doubt she can forgive you. Do yourself and her a favor and just let her go. She's building a new life there, let her be happy." Said Bert and continued his work. David left but knew that if he could only talk to her, he could ask for forgiveness.

"Live Well clinic, this is Celia. Yes Mrs Bernt, you have an appointment tomorrow morning at 3:30 pm. Of course, myself and the nurse on call will be there. Yes, thank you."

Today Celia was going through some appointment that needed extra help, besides being a therapist, she was also going through the ones that needed prescriptions.

A delivery came through the door, and she let him in, it was a flower delivery "Hi, can I help you?" The young guy looked at the paper and asked "Celia Caceres? I have a delivery for you, sign here please?" She looked surprised and signed the receipt, gave him a 5-dollar bill, and let him out the door. The flowers, a bouquet of red roses with a single white in the middle had a card. She took it out to read, it only said "Look out the door."

For a moment she thought it was a joke, there wasn't anyone there. Through the elevator door, a man came out. It wasn't someone she knew though, but she let him in "Hi, can I help you?" The man, very handsome and dark haired said "I see you got the flowers, maybe I can introduce myself. I'm Joseph Andrews and I work downstairs in the security department for the NYPD. I've been seeing you for a few months and thought that we could get to know each other, if you want of course."

Celia was surprised by the man; he was nice and handsome but she wasn't looking for someone new. Although he did have a nice touch with the flowers. She smiled, shook his hand and said "Thank you, they're beautiful, I'm Celia Caceres, I work as chief therapist here at Live Well clinic. Nice to meet you, Joseph."

The guy was charming, no doubt about that but still it felt like she was betraying David. She removed the thought from her mind and showed him that he could take a seat, they talked for a while, laughed even. Joseph had kind eyes, a nice smile, and a great sense of humor. He didn't look at all like David, his eyes were blue, and he had a slighter darker voice.

"So, I was thinking that we could go for a bite and then watch the Lakers game? They're playing tonight at Madison if you're into basketball of course." He said in an interested voice, and Celia nodded a yes. "I'll pick you up at 7 then, I know this great place that serves the best steak. You're not vegan, are you?" She laughed, said that the steak would be great, and they parted ways.

She continued with work; it was only 1 pm in the afternoon. As the time for her dinner with Joseph was approaching, her heart was racing. 6:30 pm and now she was nervous, but checked her clothes, fixed her hair, closed the door, and locked. Joseph was by the entrance, smiled big when he saw her and came over to greet her: "Hey, you okay? Ready?" Celia smiled and he opened the door for her, they walked into the New York night.

"It was a very nice evening, thank you Joseph, for everything." said Celia as they were standing by Times Square saying goodnight. Joseph leaned in to give her a kiss on the cheek, she was blushing, and he moved his head towards her lips instead. It was a soft one, a light touch between them and he smiled "Please, call me Joe and you're one marvelous woman Celia. Can I, walk you to your apartment? It's not the safest neighborhood."

He stretched out his hand and she took it with certain doubt, she had dated others before but it didn't feel right. It was always awkward to hold hands with someone who didn't do anything for your heart but this, she hadn't felt this in a long time, with David. It would seem like she was finally ready to move on.

Joe held her hand as they walked towards her apartment, passed a few parks until they reached hers. They were standing outside, and he kissed her again, this time a little more intense than before. He left her breathless and suddenly they were entering her building, kissing. She opened the door, while he has kissing her neck and threw the keys on the table. Joe shut the door behind him, and they continued, he removed his jacket and tie, threw them on the floor. He opened the zipper to her dress and slowly took it off her, she closed her eyes, feeling him touch her carefully over her bare shoulders to remove her bra. She turned around to kiss him, removed his shirt and he scooped her up in his arms to the bed.

Joe was well built, had a nice body and extraordinarily strong. Celia got lost in his kisses and the beautiful things he whispered to her. She had never had sex with someone she only met once but somehow it felt normal, it was like she always knew him.

Sunlight woke Celia up; she had forgot to close the curtain. She stretched herself and saw a man lay in her bed, Joe was still very much asleep.

She didn't regret last night, it was nice to feel attractive and desired by a man like Joe. As she moved closer to him, he turned around and saw her, smiled big, said "Mm good morning" and leaned in to kiss her. Celia put her head on his chest and listen to his heartbeat, he stroked her bare back bringing chills in the heat.

"Do you want some breakfast? I make some mean pancakes!" he said and caressed her face, she leaned in to kiss him again to respond, "Can the pancakes wait?" He pulled her on top of him and they continued what they started the night before.

It was a beautiful Saturday morning, well not morning anymore, more like lunch time. It was Celia's day off and Joe was making pancakes in her kitchen in his boxers.

They had talked in bed for some time before getting up as well: he had been single for 10 years, no kids and lived close to Madison Square. He worked security for NYPD for 15 years, before that he was a security guard at the Natural History Museum for 5 years. He wasn't a new yorker, from Chicago and no parents. Has a half-brother and a half sister, both live in California where he spends his summer vacations surfing.

Celia told him about her past, about her life in Birmingham and then London, that she was engaged but it didn't work out. He looked worried at her since it still affected her but kept his arms around her to comfort her.

After breakfast and a shower, yes, they shared that shower, they went for a walk in Central Park. It was a quiet day; most people were at the mall or the movies, so they had the park to themselves.

They stopped by his apartment: a big penthouse with a big living room and tv, an even bigger bed and a great kitchen. Since he was a cooking afficionado, he loved being there more than the tv room. He made her a great late lunch and enjoyed the dessert in the bedroom.

CHAPTER 14:
WEDDING PLANS PART 2

Joe and Celia spent almost every day together, they grew close as a couple and soon celebrated their first year together. They had talked about moving in together, buying a place that would be theirs rather than just his and hers. Joe had a friend in real estate and left word to let him know that he was looking. Since Celia only knew Bert and he had connections all over, but he had already done so much for her that she really didn't want to ask.

Days before, Joe had in secret bought an engagement ring to Celia. He couldn't think of any other worthy than Cartier: a rose gold band with the words "Love is forever" in Cezanne style. He was eager to give it to her on their anniversary.

Celia was in her office when the flowers arrived by messenger, red roses in 4 bouquets. She was thrilled to see them and have their smell spread across the room. Inside one of the bouquets, there was a note: "To the only woman who made me smile, Love Joe". She sent him a text: "Thank you for the flowers, the smiles and this year filled with love. I love you, C <3". He sent her a wink back with a kiss.

She looked out the window and thought of David, not with sadness but with a certainty that everything was said and done. They had not spoken in years, and she imagined him happy with Tamara and their daughter. Celia felt at peace with their parted ways.

Later that day, on her way home, she met Joe by the entrance. He was waiting for her; "Hello my dear, how was your day?" They kissed and walked home to her apartment. Upstairs she looked in the fridge to see what they could have for dinner.

"Shall I cook something, or do you want take-out?" Joe was sitting in the chair by the kitchen, she liked it when he sat across it like a bad-ass cop. There was something sexy about it. "How about neither? Let's just go out for dinner, I know just the place."

They went out to the steakhouse, the same from their first date but to her disappointment it was closed. "Oh that's a bummer, want to go someplace else?" she said, and he nodded a no, walked to the side, finding an open door. "Welcome honey, please after you. Watch your step." he said and let her in, suddenly the lights turned on just enough to create a romantic ambiance.

A man in white chef coat came to greet them, Joe gave him a hug and presented him "Hey man, thank you for doing this. Celia, this is Gianni, the best chef in town. Gianni, my friend, this is my girlfriend, Celia. He'll be cooking for us tonight honey, he makes a mean pasta dish!"

Celia was amazed to see the restaurant in a whole new light: a single table with candles and roses and music. He drew out the chair for her, offered some lemon iced tea while Gianni brought the food: a selection of risottos, side dishes and pasta.

It smelled fantastic and she could not think of a more thoughtful gift for their anniversary.

As they talked, laughed, and exchanged endearments, it was time for desserts. Before she tasted the gelato, Joe got up and stood beside her "I know a year isn't much but it's enough to know that you, Celia, are the one. I offer not only my life but also my love, my fidelity, my earthly possessions, and my heart. Everything is yours if you marry me Celia, I love you. Please, marry me."

The Cartier box was placed on the table, and he shyly opened it up for her to see and be surprised. She was immensely happy, to the difference from her past failed relationship. "Yes, I do Joseph. Yes, yes, yes!!" She threw herself onto him and he grabbed her waist, spinning her around. They kissed, hugged and Joe took out the ring. She saw the inscription and couldn't hold back the tears: he knew that Cezanne handwriting was her favorite and for her it meant a lot to know that he remembered such detail.

"I love you, and I truly want to marry you as soon as you desire." He said to her ear, and she cried. "What is it? Why are you crying?" he whispered, sitting her on his lap. "I'm just so happy, I didn't think I could ever be again. And here you are, the man of my dreams, who's going to be my husband."

Joe kissed her, hugged her, and whispered "I'll love you for as long as I live, and even after, you will be forever the love of my life." Now he was crying too, so they had some gelato before heading home.

At Celia's apartment, Joe was sitting with her in the couch. "What do you think of a Christmas wedding? City hall, a few friends and family, then a big dinner at Gianni's?"

Celia was convinced by his idea, it looked beautiful in theory and the only thing that could be needed was to fly her family to New York. So, she decided "It sounds perfect sweetie, in 2 months from now, we'll be married."

CHAPTER 15:
WEDDING DAY

I, Joseph Eric Andrews take thee Celia Andrea Caceres to be mine forever and always as my wife. In all moments, good or bad, I'll be there, as long as we both shall live." He placed the rose gold band on her left ring finger and kissed it. "I, Celia Andrea Caceres take thee Joseph Eric Andrews to be my husband, the man I love and honor forever and always." Together they said "I promise you fidelity, love and strength through the challenges ahead. To be with you is to love you."

The city hall official wiped a tear from her eye and said "Well, after such beautiful vows, by power invested in me from the state of New York declare you husband and wife. You may kiss the bride and please folks, give it up for Mr. and Mrs. Andrews-Caceres!"

Everybody present cheered, but in their moment, nothing could be heard. It was like they were alone in that moment, just existed for each other when they kissed. The sound came back, and they hugged their families, all happy for their sake.

A small party for their family and friends at Gianni's reminded more of a family dinner. There was laughter, happiness, and great company. "A toast for the lovely couple, and now let's dance!" said Celia's dad and the DJ played "Save the last dance". "Wife, want to dance?" Joe said and picked up his wife, she took his hand and they danced.

"So, what have you prepared for me? I must warn you, the plane leaves at 10:30 am to our honeymoon so we can't oversleep. Baby, are you…Wow." He said until he saw her coming out of the bathroom. Celia was wearing a purple satin nightgown; she was a beautiful vision. Joe went over to take her hand and said "Well Mrs. Andrews, you never cease to amaze me. You look absolutely divine…" The night was beautiful, it was devotion written all over it. He carefully removed one strap from her shoulder at the time, kissed her shoulders and removed the nightgown completely. Joe then let her remove his blue shirt, pants and slept in each other's arms.

The arrival to the Maldives was a bit messy, Celia was tired from the 22-hour trip and Joe was so hyperactive after the exposure to 40 degrees in direct sunlight.

Luckily, their hotel room on the 10th floor had AC. Joe put their luggage by the wall towards the bathroom and scooped Celia up in his arms, she giggled and said "It's beautiful, how long are we staying?"

He put her down gently and said "Well, here we're staying a week, then we're flying to Tokyo, stay 2 weeks there and then off to Bali for a week. Since it's my first vacation in years, I thought this could be the best opportunity to spend time with my wife. We both need to be alone together."

She moved closer and pulled herself closer in his arms, burying her nose in his chest and whispered, "A whole month just you and me travelling, how can I go back to work then?"

Joe laughed; he was very ticklish. He sat her down on

the bed, laid her down, opened a few buttons from her blouse and began kissing her. Celia took a deep breath and felt how aroused she was by his touch; she placed her hand on his cheek and followed with a finger along his jawline. He smiled and gave her a kiss on the lips, before saying "Before we continue this rather ravishing moment, I have to tell you a secret." Celia got nervous, what could it possibly be? She sat up but didn't close her blouse, he caressed her neck and grabbed his phone from his jacket.

"I got word from my friend from the real estate, he found us a house. I know that we both should look at it, but I'm quite sure this is us. Here, let me show you." He said and opened the phone, in his gallery there was a beautiful house. It looked like a mansion with 2 floors, nice vegetation and what it looked like a beach in the background.

Celia was surprised but it was a happy surprise "It's beautiful, where is this? Is there a part of New York that I don't know about?"

He smiled, like he was carrying this big secret, he took both her hands and said "It's the Hamptons, you know a lot of celebrities and fancy people live there during the summer. But in the winter, it's even more beautiful. I know it's far from the office but I'll be driving you there and home, you never have to think that you must take that hideous train again. It's ours if you want it. What do you think?"

Celia tried to wrap her mind around that big house, to be living in the Hamptons close to the beach. She was teary, laughed a little and said "It's perfect, yes of course I want to live there. I'll be living with you and that's all I want. I love it, and I love you." They kissed, Joe was all welled up, but Celia knew what could cure is happy tears. She sat in his lap, removed his shirt, and kissed his neck. He groaned, pulled her up in his arms to change positions. Both fell on the bed and laughed about it, but instead of continuing Joe said "Can we save this for tonight? I really want to go swimming with you and have some dinner, what do you think?"

It sounded like a great idea, so she agreed. It was after all the Maldives outside.

30 degrees in the water was more than enough, it covered up the extreme heat in the air and made it bearable to be outside. The ocean was clear blue, many fishes swimming from here to there. It felt like an aquarium though, like when she was little, and she always wanted to swim with them. Almost like a mermaid.

"You seem like a great swimmer; did you take classes?" he said, admiring her technique. She smiled, maybe she just was a fish in another life. "Well, sort of. When I was in 2nd grade my school had mandatory swimming classes, then when I was a scout, I also learned to swim in the ocean, hang upside down from a canoe and got bumped in the head with a mast when we sailed through a storm. Besides, most girls back then really wanted to be mermaids." Celia said and got out of the water, Joe came right after and helped her with the towel.

"Thank you honey, wow is it hot here. Think we can have some lunch now?" she said, and Joe helped her up. They found this great place to eat with AC by the table, enjoyed some steak and potatoes besides each other's company.

It was almost evening, and it was time to rest in the hotel, Celia couldn't stay awake and went straight to bed after her shower. Joe kept her company for a while, texting with the real estate guy. Apparently, they weren't the only ones interested but Joe told him to score that house, it was particularly important to his wife.

"I'm sure your father could help you out man, after all he is Bert Jameson, the psychiatrist mogul of the rich and famous in New York." Joe frowned upon the reminder; his father was estranged to him until he was a teenager so in theory, he meant nothing. He didn't need Celia to know that his father was also her boss, the same that helped her all this time.

He watched her sleep, she looked perfect in her sleeping gown. It wasn't her fancy one she wore on their wedding night but a more home-like one. "How could a woman be so perfect, only God knew why they had crossed paths in the hallway. To think that she chose me when she could've had anyone." he thought to himself. It was now 3 am and he still couldn't sleep, he got carefully out of bed and stood by the window. Joe got on his knees and prayed "God in heaven, I thank you for these moments I get to live with my baby. She means the world to me and is the only person I care about, please lord let her stay. I know I haven't been the forgiving son I should with my father but I'm not as mighty as you. Please give me strength to be the man she needs. Amen."

As he was getting up, Celia put her hand on his bare

shoulder and got down next to him. She had heard the last part of his prayer and gave him a hug "I'm not going anywhere, I promise. Come back to bed, let's get some sleep, okay?" He got up and scooped her up, put her gently underneath the covers and got in next to her. "Goodnight baby, sweet dreams."

CHAPTER 16:
TOKYO

Welcome to Haneda Airport, please remain seated until the plane has parked entirely by the terminal. When opening the overhead compartments please be aware of falling items. If you have any connecting flights, contact the cabin crew. Thank you for flying with JAL and we wish you a pleasant trip here in Tokyo Japan. Arigato."

It had been 2 weeks since they were in the Maldives and now had touchdown in Tokyo, Japan. Joe was still asleep; he had been rather worried lately. He received texts from someone he called "DON'T BOTHER" and this person called him "Son".

She didn't want to pry, but at some point, she would need to ask him who it was. Carefully she placed a kiss on his cheek, and he woke up "Hey sweetheart, everything okay? How long until we're in Tokyo?". Celia smiled to him and showed him the window, the plane was just parking "You surely slept all the way, are you okay?" Joe smiled, kissed her, and told her "You kept me awake the other night, I think I'm still recovering."

She blushed, yes, they indeed had an exceptionally good vacation and lately sleeping together was more than important. Not that he complained, he loved it that she could take charge in the sexual matter. Celia was a queen, and she knew how provocative she could be so her husband would give in to her enchantments.

"Where are we staying?" she said as they deboarded the plane, he checked his phone "Uh it's called, difficult spelling… Uh… Shibuya?" he said and gave her a big smile, she recognized the name.

Her sister had been there on her honeymoon with Patrick, she studied Japanese so for her it was a piece of cake.

At the Shibuya Excel Hotel Tokyu there was a huge room waiting for them, it was like a whole apartment. Celia put down the bags, checked the bathroom and ended up in front of their balcony. The whole prefecture of Tokyo could be seen from this hotel, it was a vision, and she was incredibly happy to see it with Joe.

He was in the bathroom, apparently, he didn't feel so good after eating a yogurt at 3 am. She knocked on the door "Babe, how are you feeling? Want me to get you some sparkly water?" Joe was red in the face, but he wasn't sick in his stomach. He was crying.

"I can't do this baby, I, I can't…" he fell on his knees by her waist and grabbed her. She held onto him, to comfort him and asked "Hey, hey what's going on? What can't you do? Is it me? You don't want me anymore?" she was concerned, but he nodded. "No no baby, you're the only one. The only one I care about, no one else. I. I must tell you something and I don't really know how you'll take it. Come, sit down with me."

They sat together in the bathroom, he wrapped his arms around her waist and put his head on her shoulder. He took a deep breath and began "My mom died when I was 17 years old, I grew up in New York with my aunt that later died. So, I tend for myself until now.

A few years ago, a man contacted me and said that he was my father, something I had to check with DNA test and all. His name is Bert, and he's your boss. I didn't know about him knowing you until he told me that there was a young woman that he saw as his daughter that took over his office here in New York. When I saw you, I thought you were someone else. I swear, I didn't know who you were. I fell in love with you, you fell in love with me and now he tells me when I tried to buy the house in the Hamptons that he's willing to give it to us because of you. I accepted, because I knew you wanted something beautiful, and I wanted to give it to you. I'm sorry I didn't tell you, please Celia, don't leave me."

Celia was silent, she just listened to what he just said and held on to him tightly. Maybe that's why Bert sent her there, to meet his son, a wonderful man that now is her husband. She turned around to face him and placed her hands on his cheeks "Listen to me Joe, to me you're my husband. If you're Bert's son or not, it doesn't matter because I love you. The man you are, how you feel for me, how you made me love you and what we've lived so far. Bert is important to me but he's also my boss, if he couldn't take care of you well, it's his loss. Come on, let me make you some tea."

They sat by the window, with the AC on. The humidity in Tokyo was extreme during the summer period, but it worked simply fine with the AC at full speed.

Joe was pensive, his eyes wouldn't face hers and she realized how unlike Bert he was: He had brown eyes, small freckles on his nose that could only be seen in certain light, a little shark fin like nose, but his kindness you could only tell from his way of being.

He still had tears in his eyes, and Celia wanted to comfort him. She put her hand on his and he smiled towards it, still no eye contact. Quietly she moved away from him, only to stand right behind him. She wrapped her arms around him, and he held onto her, kissed her arms, and stroked them. Now she moved closer to his cheek, kissed his neck and he let out a chuckle, he grabbed her waist and now she was sitting in his lap. Joe buried his nose in her collarbone that made her laugh and he whispered, "I believe we left something hanging the other day, didn't we?"

He took her hand, lead her to the bed, she sat down, and he bent down to kiss her. She unbuttoned his belt and pants, standing there in his boxers as he removed her shirt. He then realized that she weren't wearing a bra "Well this is always a nice surprise, but how?" She showed him the inside, it had an inserted sports bra so she wouldn't need to wear extra underneath. He laughed, threw the shirt on the floor, and pulled her up to his embrace. His kisses covered her neck, chest, and belly. The need was there, she felt it every time he kissed her, it was almost like he was afraid to lose her if he let go.

"You know something, we could probably stay longer in Bali if you want. Buy a house there, maybe work from home or even start a new business. What do you think?" he said as he stroked a hair lock from her face. Celia turned to face him, gave him a deep sigh and replied "I know what this is, you don't want to go back to New

York. Is it because of Bert? He never comes to the office, usually just meetings through Google. You've got nothing to worry about honey."

Joe stroked her face; his wife couldn't think ill of anyone, not even the man who's helped her all this time all the way to New York. But it wasn't her fault, that's one of the reasons he loved her: her kindness. He leaned in for a kiss, it was soft and sweet, like when they kissed for the first time. "I don't really mind where I live, I just know that I want to live with you. Now, maybe we should have something to eat. Do you think they make pancakes here?"

CHAPTER 17:
CHANGES

It had been a few days to get back into normal lifestyle. After being in places like the Maldives, Tokyo and then Bali it was hard to back to normal office hours.

Lately it was hard for Celia to be away from Joe, he had become her magnet. He wasn't the kind to say no either, he was more than obliged to his wife.

Late Wednesday afternoon, Celia was going through some paperwork in the office when she remembered a particular evening in Bali:

They had just had dinner by the beach, with live music around them and the ambiance was just seducing. They danced, laughed and suddenly he whispered in her ear: "Can we just go back to the room, you look exquisite." In the house hut, they slammed into pretty much everything: walls, closets until they reached the bed. Joe basically tore her island inspired dress but she didn't care, his shirt she tore off on the way in. He kissed her feverish, she was out of breath and together they moaned into each other.

She smiled to herself, before Joe and well David, she had never been inclined to sex. Most girls in their early 20's are sexually active but she didn't do anything until when she dated David. He was experienced, so he kind of taught her what was to expect when you were in an adult relationship.

It didn't feel weird being with him either, it was right in that moment. But Joe, her husband, he was the one that ignited her fire.

She called him "Hey honey, what time can you get off work? Me too, I think it was Bali. Yes, yes. Okay pick me up in 30 minutes. Can't wait. Forget about dinner, okay we can order in. Love you, bye."

Celia had fallen asleep, and Joe was admiring her, there was something they had never spoken off: having children. So much sex they've had during the year, it's strange that she never gotten pregnant. He checked her medicines since she was a type 1 diabetic but nothing of birth control. He laid by her side, listened to her silent breath, and decided to ask her the next morning about expanding their little family.

During breakfast, he popped the question: "Baby, there's something I needed to ask you. You know I love you, and I hope you don't take this the wrong way but how come after all sexy fun we've had and will have that you haven't got pregnant?"

Celia was by the kitchen, fixing the last piece of toast. She took a deep breath and said with a calm voice "I should've told you this before but I guess I was scared about how you would react. I can't have children, I'm barren."

Joe was devastated, not because he couldn't be a biological father but that his wife had carried this alone.

"Why didn't you tell me either way? I wouldn't judge because of that, all I think now is that you've been all alone in this. When did the doctors tell you?" He hugged her tightly and she felt his tears on her shoulders.

"It was when I was around 25 years old, I went because I've had some problems with my period. They told me it was normal and that I should just wait, then when I went again, they decided to do a check-up. They did a biopsy and told me my ovaries aren't fully developed and well, that I can't have children. But I do think adoption could be the best option, how many kids in the world that need good parents. And I actually didn't think that…" she never got to finish her sentence because Joe silenced her with a kiss. She didn't mind, but when he scooped her up in his arms and carried her to the bedroom, she said "Baby, not that I'm complaining but we have to get to work."

Joe took off his shirt, kissed her again and said "Not today, we're playing hooky. Call your office and I'll call mine, don't take too long." She sent a text to the receptionist and said, "Working from home today, call if you need anything."

She went to the bedroom and there he was on the bed, in his boxers waiting for her. Celia took off her silky robe and to his surprise she was just wearing underwear. He gave her a cheeky smile and pulled her close, smelled her CK One fragrance in her neck.

She smiled as she stroked his black hair, leaning down to kiss him. They stayed like that for a while, he caressed her stomach and kissed it, then moved up to her mouth to then pull her down the bed. "I think Mrs. Andrews that you need a new perfume, CK One is getting too ordinary. You smell like lemons, very sexy ones too." Celia laughed; he was leaving hickeys all over her chest but she didn't want him to stop. "What kind of perfume should I wear then? I've always liked the fresh lemony ones, not very much into sweet ones plus the bees chase you around."

He thought for a moment and went to check his book-case, they were still spending half time in his house and half in hers. Both had things in each other's homes so they wouldn't miss each other in case of being separated. "I got you this, went to pick up lunch and I stopped by. Hope you like it, the girl said it was feminine without being icky and hopefully bug-free."

It was a cute bag from Bloomingdale's and it contained a box from Elisabeth Arden. "Green Tea, I love this! I got it for my mom so many years ago, this one is another favorite. Aww thank you honey, I'll wear it tomorrow. There's this security guy that is crazy about me." Celia said cheeky and opened the lid, Joe made a sarcastic laughter and put the bag with perfume on the table "I'll show you security guard, come here baby."

CHAPTER 18:
HAMPTONS

What do you think? It has 4 bedrooms, kitchen, hallway, living room, garage, and garden. See that little dirt road, it goes straight to the beach. Think about it, dinner in the garden and then late-night coffee by the beach. We can have your family over, make an office so we can work from home too." Joe said and showed her around the house in the Hamptons.

Celia was happy, they would move some of his furniture here but hers didn't belong to her per se so they would stay put. She would have to send the keys back to Bert in the UK or maybe take a short trip to see her family as well. "When can we move in?" she said and Joe spun her around, showing her the keys in his hand. "How about tomorrow? I took the day off, arranged the firm to move the things you want to take with you and mine. We'll need to buy a bed though, we could do that today maybe."

"That sounds great, I do have to give back the keys to your dad, sorry to Bert. Maybe we could travel to the UK and see my family?" she said, Joe didn't mind her saying that Bert was his father. "That could be arranged babe, I have some time off, we travel together and tell your family the good news about the house."

During the afternoon they visited several bed stores looking for a good bed. Finally, the one in Bloomingdale's with memory foam and fitting pillows, a special keep cold blanket during the hot summer days and some sheets.

Joe asked the cashier for delivery to their new house in the Hamptons, arranged and done he suggested a nice dinner before heading back to her apartment.

The moving firm were loading her things into the truck, she only left the things that were already in the apartment. Joe took some photos of them there; they did have their first night in her apartment and that's something that they wouldn't forget.

"I guess this is goodbye, I'm going to miss this place. It has fond memories, don't you think?" Celia said and wiped a tear from her eye, Joe was smiling and approached to give her a hug. "Here's to a new start, you started here a little more than a year ago and now we're doing it together."

They closed the door, locked, and went downstairs to his car. "So, my place? I don't usually invite women over but you're special." he said, and Celia pinched his side.

The house was lightly furnished, their bed had arrived a few minutes before, and they were enjoying a cup of tea outside on the terrace. The evening was beautiful, lights from the center of the city could be seen from their shore and it was still too good to be true. Joe was smirking, it would seem like he was concocting a plan but wouldn't dare to tell her what. Celia took another cookie from the plate and said, "A penny for your thoughts."

He got up from his chair and kissed her, he could taste the cookie she just ate and whispered, "Want to dance?" She got up after him, the stereo was on the floor, and he connected it. There was a cd inside, one he didn't

remove: Michael Bublé's "Home". He put it on medium sound, turned down the lights a little and stretched out his hand to take hers.
"Another summer day
Has come and gone away
In Paris and Rome
But I wanna go home, mmm
May be surrounded by
A million people I
Still feel all alone
Just wanna go home
Oh, I miss you, you know
And I've been keeping all the letters
That I wrote to you
Each one a line or two
I'm fine baby, how are you?
Well, I would send them, but I know
That it's just not enough
My words were cold and flat
And you deserve more than that"

He had this beautiful singing voice; low and dark almost like an opera singer: "I could listen to you forever, singing to me like that." Joe chuckled quietly, holding onto her, stroking her back "I'll be happy to sing to you, what would you like to hear?" She thought for a moment, closed her eyes, and said, "Do you know any song from The Phantom of the Opera?"

He thought for a moment and found the exact right one: Music of the night. He hummed quietly as he held her tighter, she kept her eyes closed and found the lullaby quite relaxing. She must have fallen asleep, because when she woke up it was almost 3 am and Joe was sleeping right next to her. He was snoring, something she got used to, but he was appealing in any way, his messy hair on the pillow, the wrinkle he did like he was focusing on something and his muscular arms grabbing the sheets. Celia got carefully out of bed, trying not to wake him up. She went to the bathroom and got back, still asleep but now she wanted him to wake up.

She removed her shirt and pants and carefully placed a kiss on his lips. He didn't notice it, she tried again but this time a little bolder: she placed her hand on his chest, caressed him, counted some freckles she could see in the moonlight that entered their bedroom. Still nothing, now she moved towards him instead, climbed on top. He woke up an hour later and to his surprise, she had fallen asleep on his chest. He chuckled as he moved her back to her side of the bed, this time she noticed him. "No, no babe, go back to sleep. It's only 4:30 am, we don't have to get up until 10."

Even though she was still sleepy, she knew exactly what she wanted "I tried to wake you up at 3 because I wanted to sleep with you, but I think I got too tired."

Joe said nothing, instead he leaned in to kiss her but instead pulled her on top of him. He held onto the outside of her thigh with one hand and put the other one behind his head, his eyes showed admiration for her. She laid down on his chest and he wrapped the sheets around her, it didn't take long until she fell asleep again.

CHAPTER 19:
VISIT FROM THE PAST

Uh, Celia, there's a man here who wants to see you." Said the receptionist on the intercom. Celia smiled, for a moment she thought it could be Joe coming for their mutual lunch hour. "Is it my husband, show him right in Kelly. Thanks." There was a tone in her voice, like uncertainty "No Celia, he said his name is David."

Celia dropped the notepad on the floor, it was a name she hadn't heard in an awfully long time. She hesitated before replying "Send him in please Kelly, can you bring some refreshments as well?" The door opened and there he was, David, the only other man in her life that came and made an impact, then left just as quickly.

"Celia, it's been a while. How are you?" he said, the same kind voice she always known. He looked well, happy but she couldn't tell if he was happy to see her only or just generally happy.

"It surely has, how is everything? How's Ally? And Tamara?" she said and showed him the chair, to take a seat. Her receptionist, Kelly, knocked on the door with iced tea and cookies. She left the tray and Celia nodded a thank you.

David sat down, poured iced tea into the 2 glasses and said "Ally's fine, she's grown. Tamara, well, we left it there, we only have words when it comes to Ally and me well, I miss you. Our life together in London, I came to ask you to come back. I know it's been 2 years, but I still love you."

He handed the glass to her, and she took it, then he noticed the ring on her finger. He grabbed her hand and looked closer, then he knew "You're married, you got married?! How could you do this? Here I am pouring my heart out and you found yourself another guy??" Celia dropped the glass on the floor and David kept pulling, someone entered and pushed him away "Let her go!"

Joe had entered and fought off David from Celia, who was rubbing off the pain from her wrist. "I don't know who you are but get out or I'll make you!" said Joe and was ready to throw out David.

"Joe, calm down. It's David, my ex-fiancé. David, this Joe, my husband." She said and held out her arms to keep them apart, Joe realized that this was the one guy Celia had dated and almost married.

"I'm sorry but even so, it's no way of treating her. Honey, you're sure he didn't hurt you?" Joe said and checked her hand to see if there was a bigger damage, then went to look for a broom to sweep up all the glass pieces on the floor.

David had calmed down, he finished his glass with tea and said "Well I guess we don't have anything else to talk about Celia, I'm sorry I disturbed you and your husband. Oh, and the hand, I'm sorry about that too. Goodbye."

Celia nodded and he left, Joe met him in the hallway when he came with the broom. He saw her looking sad and he asked "Are you okay? Did he hurt you?" She went to his side, hugged him and cried "I'm okay, I'm glad you were here. I've never seen him so mad, we parted ways ages ago and now he wants me back."

Joe comforted her, he was worried about the aggressive man that was her ex "Of course, you're a great woman but to his loss you're married to a non-aggressive husband instead. But if it comes to that, I'll kick his ass babe." She looked at him and he gave her a kiss on the head, sat her down by her desk while he picked up the glass.

"Thank you honey, I think I'm going to call it a day. I really need to get home and get some rest; will you be home later?" she said and gathered her things in the bag. Joe finished sweeping and replied "I have to stay, got a meeting but I'll see you home in like 3 hours. I'll bring dinner, just rest." They kissed goodbye and Celia spoke to the receptionist on the way out.

"Would you like to press charges for assault Celia?" she said, and Celia nodded "No thanks Kelly, I'm fine. I'll deal with this.". The receptionist accepted her reply and forwarded her emails so she could reply from home as well as phone calls.

As she walked out of the building, David approached her "Celia, wait." She looked nervous but remained calm, stopped, and said "David, what can I do for you?"

He gave her a weak smile; she could tell that he was ashamed. "I'm sorry, I can't believe I behaved like an animal in your office but I couldn't understand. We loved each other, at least I know I loved and still love you. You got married when you were supposed to be married to me not some other guy. I know, I made a huge mistake and now I'm paying for it. You're happy, I can see it in your eyes. When you looked at me in there, you were frightened!" She sighed, David wasn't a bad guy. They saw a bench and sat down for a moment, she began "I know how much you love me, and I still do but as my friend. We went through a lot, and I can't begin to tell you how important it was for me what we had. But I love Joe, we've grown together and he's the man I've chosen. Maybe things wouldn't have been good between you and me, later in life. Give yourself an opportunity to be happy, without me. I'm happy to stay your friend and Ally's aunt, I care for you both. I'm sorry, now I have to go." David sat with his head down, Celia patted his hand gently and saw that he was crying, she moved closer to hug him.

"I know, she cares for you too. She's with Tamara, but she told me to give you this. I'll always love you, you know. I'm hope he makes you happy, I know I should've." He said and handed over a thick envelope. "Thank you, I'll be going back to Birmingham for vacations to my family. I'll let you know so you can bring her over. Take care David, I love you too." Celia said and they parted ways. It wasn't a relief but it felt much better than before, it was a chapter that needed closure.

At home Celia was finishing the last dishes, Joe still hadn't come home. She dried her hands and opened the envelope she had gotten from Ally via David.

"Babe, I'm home. Babe? Hey, what happened?" Joe said and found his wife crying in the couch, he went over quickly and put his arms around her. "I'm fine, I just got a letter and some drawings from David's daughter. I miss her, she's a great kid." She said and curled up in his arms, he kissed her head and took the letter to read it.

"Well, what's not to love. You're a great woman, I've told you before and you'll make a great mum to any kid really, when did you get this?" he said after looking at the drawings and letter.

She sighed, wiped her tears and replied "As I left the building, David was waiting outside. We talked, he apologized due his overreacting and he gave me this. We've parted ways as friends." Joe seemed concerned and she continued "We hugged it out, I told him that when I go back to Birmingham, I would give him a call so he can bring Ally over. I also told him, that me marrying you was something I chose to do because I love you. I love him too, just as my friend nothing more. What we had, it ended there, and he understood."

Joe hugged her, put the content of the envelope on the table and took her hand. He led her to the bedroom and said, "Tell me again, what did you say?" He had this look in his eyes, lust, and love so she told him "That I chose you because I love you."

She spoke with a soft voice; he closed his eyes for a short moment like he was savoring the moment and he proceeded to undress her. Celia let him, they had been through a roller coaster of emotions and now she just wanted to enjoy her husband.

"I won't let anyone harm you and I'm happy to hear you say that you love me so much. I love you, Celia." He whispered as he took of his t-shirt and laid her on the bed, Joe covered her naked body with kisses before they made love.

"Hey, I'm trying to reply to the emails from work. Ha-ha stop it, I can't write. Joe! Look, now I have to retype this." Celia said between laughter, while Joe kept kissing her neck and tickle her. "I don't want you to work, pay attention or I'll make it worse." He said and bit her softly in her earlobe. She finished retyping the email and turned to him, he was sitting on the bed with nothing more than his boxers. "Lucky I don't have a patient, I wonder if my male patients would appreciate a naked therapist in their sessions." She said and got up from the computer chair, putting her arms around his shoulders, pushing him onto the bed. "Trying to be funny huh? I'll show you funny." He said and moved her on her back, kissed her neck until she felt his tongue tickle her collarbone. She stroked his black hair, pressed a kiss on his lips and he smiled, stroking her chin. "I can't get tired of this, us like this." He whispered, she had placed her head on his chest and stroked him, they held a synchronized breathing before he said, "Do you think we can have some dinner, or shall we stay like this for another half hour?"

Celia looked up to him and said, "We can stay for 15 minutes and then have some dinner, although we don't have anything in the fridge." Joe leaned in, kissed her, and replied "Well, lucky for us, there's delivery food."

CHAPTER 20:
JOURNEY HOME

Before your biological dad died, did you have any contact?" said Joe, Celia was looking out the window over the massive ocean underneath. They were on a British Airways on their way to Birmingham, to see her family. She thought for a moment and said "Well, we did spend some time together once a year, 2 years in a row. He lived in Spain, Barcelona to be precise and well I went there for the summer. At first it was all good but then I realized why my mom left him in the first place, he was a deadbeat, pardon the pun but it's true. He didn't give me anything besides heartache and I don't mean material stuff, he left us just like that and then he was demanding things from me. Like I owed him when it truly was the other way around."

Joe found it heartbreaking to hear her like that, cold but also incredibly sad. He held her hand, moved it to his chest and said "If we have kids, adopted or not, I'm not letting them down. In fact, they'll probably hate me for being so close to them but I'll be there and for you as well. I cannot understand men like that, runaway fathers. Well kind of like my own, it's strange that he cares about others."

He realized that the comment was directly to her, he shook his head "I'm sorry honey, I don't mean it like that. What I mean is…" Celia smiled "I know what you mean, don't apologize. Yes, it's true.

How can a man care just like that when his own child didn't even have the possibility to say something about it? Bert has been good to me but he's still my boss. I work for him."

Joe put his hand on her face to move her closer, they kissed, and she fell asleep on his shoulder.

"Celiaaaaaa!!!! Welcome home sis, God I've missed you so much! How are you?" said Claire, who picked them up from the airport. They hugged, the kids were at home with her husband and their grandparents. They talked a little and she greeted Joe as well, when he went for a suitcase wagon, she asked "You know we had Ally over a week ago, she asked about you. Have you talked to David?" Celia gathered the bags and saw Joe coming with the wagon "Yeah, he actually went over there, and we talked. He went a little insane and got into an argument with Joe, but we parted as friends, I told him that I love my husband. But we could stay friends and I'll check on Ally when I'm here."

"I think he still loves you, when he dropped off Ally, he told Patrick that he wanted to win you back. But I had no idea that he went there." Claire said and helped Celia with the bags.

"It doesn't matter since we've parted as friends, but I care of course. He's not a bad guy, he just needs time." She said and they went all to the car.

At home they family waited anxiously to see their daughter again, it was difficult to have her live so far away from them.

"Celia, we've missed you so much!!" said her mom and dad, when she hugged both. They greeted Joe, just as warmly. "Mr. and Mrs. Caceres, we've missed you too. Since we don't want to intrude, I've booked a hotel for the upcoming 2 weeks we're here."

Celia's mom and dad, were simply happy to have them there but accepted their need for privacy. They greeted Claire and Patrick's kids, noticing that Claire looked a little rounder than before. "Claire, I don't want to be rude but, are you?" Celia began and Claire giggled "Yes, I'm pregnant. 3 months now, we're having our third baby sis. What about you? Will you be adopting or something?"

Celia smiled, they hadn't talked any more than she could be the best mom ever but other than that nothing. "I think we're just being together for now and frankly I'm okay with it. But tell me, is the baby planned or?" Claire was happy, telling her all about it.

After a nice dinner, loads of laughter and anecdotes, Celia and Joe were finally at the hotel. "Babe, I'm going to shower, would you uh, care to join me?" he said from the bathroom. She raised her eyes and noticed that he was standing in the doorway, naked.

"Sir, you're not making it easy for me." She went to his side, and he went in after her. The bathtub was big enough for both, he was massaging her shoulders and Celia was falling asleep.

"You're tired, want to rinse?" he said and took off the plug from the tub. She nodded, couldn't stay awake. Joe turned on the shower and helped her quickly, took one of the big towels to wrap her in. "Come on honey, watch your step. There we go, now I don't mind you are sleeping naked." He put the sheets on her, and she curled up to the side, he picked up a smaller towel to put underneath her head. "Goodnight honey, love you." He whispered and curled up next to her.

After 2 weeks of spending time with family, it was time to travel back to the US. Celia had also had some time with David's daughter Ally, they went to the park with Claire and the kids and even to the movies with Joe. Ally was unsure about him in the beginning but then she understood how nice and thoughtful he was, she suggested that he and her dad could be friends. Something Joe didn't mind, he said to Ally "Tell your dad, next time he's in New York, I'll buy him a beer." They hugged; Celia was incredibly happy to see them become friends.

Airport bound, this time they took a cab. She admired the view of her hometown, before boarding the plane to her new home with her husband. "You okay honey? You've been quiet the whole ride here, do you want to postpone the trip home, spend more time with your family?" Joe said, stroking her back.

Celia seemed to have woken up from her quietness, she moved towards Joe's embrace and said "No honey, I'm fine. It's just odd to leave them again and come back in a few months again, they're not 2 hours away anymore."

Joe kissed her head, took her hand, and walked around in the terminal while waiting for boarding. Within the hours they boarded the American Airlines bound for New York.

"Feels good to be home, it's hot here, isn't it? I'm going to open a window, put the bags in the corner honey, I'll unpack them later. Want to take a bath or a shower perhaps?" he said, and Celia dropped the bags by one side, she washed her hands in the smaller toilet before answering "Oh a shower sounds nice, but you know, we could take a swim in the ocean first. What do you think?"

Joe nodded towards her and took off his pants, he kept the boxers and said "We don't really need bathing suits right, it works well with just your underwear and mine. Shall we?"

The breeze was perfect in that hot day, they walked to the beach and went into the water. It must have been a few hours of playing more than swimming when she said "Okay, now I'm hungry and tired. Do you think we have some food in the freezer?"

Joe took her hand and led her out of the water. She took the towel and dried a little, wrapped herself in and he shook his head to dry. Sometimes he was just a kid, she laughed at him, and they walked inside. He turned on the shower with tempered water, went out naked and said, "Your bath is ready ma'am, please allow me to escort you." She laughed even more, went through her drawer to find some clothes when he showed up behind her, kissed her neck and whispered, "You don't need clothes, I'll be happy to have you walk around naked."

Celia laughed, turned around to kiss him properly "You would like that huh? I still must find clothes, it's better to have at least underwear. Can you put the AC on please?" Joe did a salute and went to turn on the

AC, went back to his wife who was now waiting in the bathroom.

"Have you realized that we haven't argued once since we got married? If you don't count that time when you got mad at me for not letting you watch your tv-series." He said, stroking her bare back. Celia and Joe laid in bed after the shower, just talking as they usually did. She thought for a moment, then said "Well that wasn't an argument, I was just annoyed really. But come to think of it, no, we haven't. Maybe we just work well together, right?" She leaned in to kiss him, he held onto her and said "Yeah we do, maybe it's because we're very much alike in sense of thinking and priorities. I'm not much into arguing actually, unnecessary when you can talk to the person, make love to that person, then make her do you bidding?"

She chuckled in his mouth, intensified their kiss and he said "Well, kind of, you're the one that tells me what to do and I'm happy to oblige. Like now for instance, I'm not going to say no to a beautiful woman who wants to sleep with me."

Celia climbed on top of him and said, "You better not, besides, I can be very persuasive you know." He laughed a little and grabbed her waist, pushed her towards him. They held each other for a while, she was falling asleep on his chest. He turned over, letting her on the bed and stayed nose to nose with her. Both were tired, after taking that long swimming round that they fell asleep.

CHAPTER 21: RESOLUTIONS

Celia was going through old photos and found one from her marriage with Joe. They had a good 5 years together and he died far too young, today it marked exactly 6 months.

It was one of those days that you'd rather forget, car accident on his way to work. A truck with wood crossed his path, some of the load fell onto his car and he didn't even see it coming. The phone call to her office was the worst, Kelly, the receptionist received it because Celia was out on errands and when she came back, she had become a widow. He died quickly, they said, apologizing for her loss. She couldn't cry, it was like they were talking about someone else. When she got home, it hit her like a brick in the head: her husband, the love of her life, had died. He left the Earth with only three words that morning when he left for work: "I love you." And somehow it felt like he was saying goodbye, because she felt certain anxiety that morning because they wouldn't be riding in together to work. She had a meeting with a patient in her office since she was not available to come to hers, Celia offered to stop by quickly and would be arriving to work later. They had agreed to have lunch instead but when he didn't call she sent a text with no reply. That's when she arrived at the office and met a devastated Kelly in the entrance, she hugged Celia, but she was far too numb to realize.

Sometime after the funeral, where her family and David plus Ally came to be supportive, she decided to sell their home in the Hamptons and go back to Birmingham. She had nothing left in New York, but she did tell Bert, Joe's estranged father to be in his memorial service. He was also devastated for his loss, thought how bad he had behaved and hoped his son had it in his heart to forgive him. Celia comforted him that Joe was a good man, in the end he wanted to give his father a chance, but he never got around to say it to his face.

The house, their home for 5 years was sold for millions, but Celia gave part of the money to her family and bought an apartment for herself. David helped her when she moved, somehow keeping her company but also to tell her that even though 5 years had passed, he still loved her like before.

She didn't have the heart to tell him off completely but did mention that she was mourning and that it would take time to heal the wounds of the loss of her husband. He stayed close, came to visit every now and then, checking in that she was doing okay. Ally did the same, she gave her the comfort she needed to stay afloat.

A letter had been forwarded to her new address in Birmingham, it was posted by Joe's lawyer: a man she briefly met a few weeks after the funeral when she contacted him about selling the house.

She opened it quickly, the tears were already running down her cheeks. To her surprise, the letter was in Joe's handwriting with no date:

Celia –wife, lover, friend:
I write this with no date, a friend told me to always have something written in case something happens. That´s why it doesn´t have a date but I did tell my lawyer in case something ever happened to me that you should have this.
I love you, Celia, I loved you since I first saw you that morning when you arrived to work. I was looking out the window and there you were, wearing a black skirt that hid those beautiful legs you have, a blouse that I kept thinking *I wonder what´s underneath* and then your smile. That´s when I knew, I should ask you out. What happened after that, well it´s just luck, I guess. I never thought you would say yes, I never thought you were brave enough to invite me in on the first night but let me tell you after that, I never wanted to leave your side. You won me over, completely and trust me to even think something might happen that would take me away from you or the other way around...it makes me sad. I never dated anyone like you, I never told you this, but I had never slept with anyone before you. I guess I was just waiting for you to come along.

You told me that sometimes guys have the wrong map on their quest to find the one girl of their dreams, well this time it was you that had the wrong map. I´ve waited for you all my life, now that I have you, I´m never leaving you again.
I´ll be your ghost, spirit, anything you need. Think of me, I´m right there.
I love you and I´ll love you until we meet again. Hopefully in a park in Heaven, I´ll be holding your favorite flower. When you see me, you´ll know.
Eternally yours,
Joe

Celia cried, all night she cried. She had never felt his loss so much as after this letter. There was a note on the envelope inside, it was from his lawyer:

Mrs. Andrews
I'm sorry for your loss once more. I'll need you to sign the following papers, it's your husbands testament. For it to be correct, you need to accept his conditions. His estate has a value of 45 million dollars, which contains his security company, 2 cars, half the house in the Hamptons and a savings account that is unlocked upon his death. You're his sole beneficiary.

Oh and Mr. Castle has received the other part of his testament and with it conditions as well. Please contact him and set up an appointment with me within 2 weeks. I'll be travelling to Birmingham next week, my numbers enclosed.
Best Regards
E. Edwards
Attorney at Law

David, Celia thought to herself, why would he be involved in this? She called him up and he was quick to answer "Hey Celi, how are you holding up? Yeah sure, I can meet. In 20? Okay, great. You know the bakery by the train station? Yeah, see you there. Bye."

He arrived a little after 3:45 pm, Celia was sitting by one of the windows. "Hey, sorry, my keys were acting up. Did you order something?" he gave her a quick kiss on the cheek and waited for her response, she nodded, lately she didn't have much appetite. "Hey, no thanks, I'm good with tea. You get something." David seemed worried, since she was paler than before, sad, and unhappy. He ordered coffee and two Danish, one jam and one with vanilla cream "Here, take this one. Your sugar levels are low, go on. So, I get that you received Joe's letter." How did he know??

"Yeah, today. It was forwarded by his lawyer, seems so spooky that it arrives today, to both of us.

He's been dead for 6 months, I can't even deal with this right now. What did he tell you?" she said and took a small piece of the Danish.

David took the other piece and said "Here, read it. I'm surprised as you are, I wasn't a fan of the guy but what he said, it moved me." He handed her the letter, written like hers but no endearments:

David:

I'm sorry to disturb your life but I hope you can put up with me this time. I'm not going to sugarcoat you: I still think you're an asshole and you don't deserve happiness with the woman I love. But if there's something I know, it's to forgive and see beyond. In a point in life, my wife loved you and you loved her, still do I think, correct me if I'm wrong. Celia is a woman you simply can't forget about and that's why I can ask you the following:

Form a family with her, don't let her be unhappy just because I'm dead. I know that you and your kid can make her happy. She

Celia's tears were running in between the anger of her husband making plans behind her back. "Now I'm pissed at you!" she thought as she looked out the window. David put his hand on hers and comforted her as she couldn't get rid of the tears that were consuming her brown eyes.

"I'm sorry, I know you're not up for anything but I guess he was looking out for you. There's something else I need to tell you: Joe was dying." David said and Celia removed her hand quickly, what was he even talking about?

He began again, "He called me about a week before his accident, told me that he needed a favor and that it involved you. I said sure, because of you. That's when he told me, he had been to the doctor about a hernia in his groin and he didn't tell you because it was probably nothing. But it was, cancer, stage 4 and that he didn't have much left. We talked and I told him to tell you the truth, he was, until that morning. I heard everything when he crashed. He made me promise not to say anything, but you know, things like this, you can't just be quiet about it. I'm sorry."

Celia got up from the chair, walked out from the coffeeshop. She was something in between mad, tired, sad and couldn't hold it together. Before hitting the ground, David was by her side.

The lights woke her up, she was uncertain where she was but by the cords and flowers on the table, a hospital. She sat up carefully, no pain but she was tired.

David came in through the door with a cup of tea and some cookies, he smiled kindly, but she remembered how mad she was him. "Why am I here?" she said, and he smiled again, he couldn't help but find her attractive when she got mad. Celia had this little wrinkle in her forehead, her eyes were darker than her usual brown and her mouth became a line.

He took a deep breath and said "Because you fainted outside the coffeeshop honey, you had one low sugar level, so they rushed you to the hospital. You're staying here for a few days and then you can go home. Want some tea, I brought cookies."

Celia gave up, she moved towards the window and couldn't hold it back anymore "Why didn't he say any-thing? Why did he marry me if he was going to leave so soon?" She cried, he couldn't take it to hear her so sad. He climbed right next to her and put his arms around her, he kissed her back and said "I'm sorry, I'm sorry that he hurt you with not saying but think of it this way: He loved you so much that he didn't want to hurt you more. This pain, what you're feeling right now, it will go away. You'll always remember him but it won't hurt anymore, I'm not going to let you be unhappy. I promised him and now I'm promising you: I'm not leaving you, ever."

They stayed like that all afternoon, her family saw them together and let them be.

When she woke up, David was sitting in the chair next to her reading.

He smiled towards her and said "Hey, how are you feeling?" She sighed, took his hand and squeezed it "I'm fine, better, I think. Have you seen my family?" He told her that they had been there and were now in the cafeteria. "You want something to eat? Drink?"

"No, thanks. It was nice, you know to sleep accompanied. I miss him so much, that's why I never wanted to fall in love with someone, because if he ever left, I don't know how to move on." She sobbed, David left his book on the chair and climbed to her bed again. He held her in his arms and comforted her pain, she moved closer to his face, and he leaned in to kiss her.

It would seem she wanted more but he stopped her gently "Sweetie, it's not that I don't want to but I think you'll regret it later. I can wait, trust me. There's nothing more in the world that I want, than to be with you again. Get some sleep, okay? I'll be here when you wake up."

CHAPTER 22:
I'LL STAND BY YOU

Celia was unpacking some things from the moving boxes; it surely had been years of constant packing and moving. Now, hopefully it was the last time. David was helping with the heavy stuff: couch, table, chairs, and bookcases.

"I think we need a break, want some tea?" she said, and he gave her a big smile "You read my mind, peach or lemon?". She smirked, came towards him with the glasses. "Lemon this time, it seems like we had all the peach ones during the move." She said and gave him the glass, sat down next to him on the floor. "I'm glad we're doing this at our own pace, no rush this time." She said after drinking half the tea, it was a hot day in the middle of the summer.

He was quiet, drank some of his and put the glass on the floor, got on his knees and put his hands around her face "I love you." She smiled, kissed the inside of his hand, and then kissed him. "Me too, I'm happy you decided to stay with me." David moved away a lock of hair that was in the way and she blushed, something she hadn't done in a while. "I like that shade." He said, she looked confused as he kissed her again, saying "The shade of pink cheeks you have, he-he." Celia laughed, hugged him, and went back to work.

A few days later, they were done decorating their new home. In one of the bookcases there was a picture from her wedding with Joe and next to it a small vase with his ashes. Half were buried in New York and the other half she took with her back to Birmingham.

David didn't mind, he sometimes put a bottle of beer next to it while he had his and talked to him. He always finished with "I'll do anything to make her happy."

Celia was falling asleep on the couch; David was finishing reading his book when he noticed. He put it down, turned off the tv and picked her up. "Come on, you need to get some sleep." She woke up and said, "I don't want to sleep." He smiled, scooped her up in his arms and whispered, "Then I think we should sleep together, if you want." She curled in his arms, and he carried her to their bedroom, the one where only she slept in as he slept on their couch. They had this arrangement since David didn't want to pressure her to sleep with him, out of respect for her late husband.

He sat her down on the bed and helped her out of her t-shirt, she removed his and pulled him close, that didn't work out so well as he fell onto her and landed on her nose. They laughed and kissed, he enjoyed the smell of rosy water on her neck and kissed it. He took off her shorts and took of his, threw them on the floor. They made love that afternoon, for the first time in over 10 years. David felt like it was just as he remembered her, so did she, it was like time had never passed. He was tender, loving and reassuring.

"Hey." He said and she opened her eyes, she had been sleeping for a few hours after. David had been watching her sleep, thinking that it could be a dream to have her back and in his bed. Well, their bed now. "Hey, how long was I asleep?" she replied, he stroked her messy hair to find her cheeks, kissed them both before finding her mouth.

"Mm…2 hours, it's nearly 6 pm, I was thinking, why don't we go out to eat? I don't want you to be working any more, you'll get tired. Quick shower and we could have some pasta in no time." He said and got out of bed, she sat up and picked up the robe from the chair. "You first? I can wait." He said and put his arms around her, she smiled and nodded.

While Celia was in the shower, David was checking his emails. He took some time off work to be with Celia a while, his new boss (he was working in a veteran hospital now) was very understanding. Celia wasn't working in Bert's company anymore, she left after Joe died and was now working in a hospital as a therapist. The pay was less but she managed, especially after the estate that Joe left her and David.

She couldn't help but sob in the shower, she still missed him very much. Could it be possible to love 2 people at the same time?

Celia got out of the shower and dressed in her robe, she went to the computer where David was sitting, putting her arms around him. "Hey, I'm going to finish this email and then hop in the shower as quickly as possible, then we go for pasta, okay?" he said, kissed her arm and got up. She removed her robe to his surprise; he gave out a quiet sigh. He grabbed her and began kissing her fervently, they moved in between kisses to the bedroom, he took her up in his arms and fell onto the bed together. He was only wearing his boxers so it wasn't much to take off, she kissed his neck and he moved to kiss hers as he entered her.

She moaned into his mouth, and he smiled, he remembered how it all began since he was her first man. He moved her on top of him and chuckled a little when she accidentally hit in over the cheek. "Sorry, are you okay?" she said in between breaths, and he just nodded. He moved her back and forth, in sync as they once did a long time ago, until they both reached satisfaction.

Celia was resting on his chest, and he stroked her back, painted with his index finger, different kinds of figures. She moved on up to face him, he smirked and said, "That was a nice surprise, I liked that." She did the same smirk and replied "It was, and I think now, it can keep happening. I think Joe's absence has left my heart, he found peace and so did I." David pulled her close, kissed her head and held onto her for a while "I think so too, he's happy, to see you happy again. He gave us his blessing."

They went out for pasta, in a new restaurant nearby. It was exceptionally good, they talked about everything and nothing, like the old days. "Hey, do you think we could, you know, go for a walk a little?" he said after dinner. He paid and they walked out, to a park nearby, where they sat by a fountain.

David put his arm around her shoulders, and they watched the water float. He moved towards her, facing her "I know I've asked before, you said yes and then things happened. I don't want to lose you again, so I'm asking, if you don't want, then I'll respect your wishes and we continue like this: lovers.

Exclusive so you don't get any ideas. Sorry, I'm extremely nervous about this. Celia, will you marry me? I know it was more than 10 years ago since I last asked, but things have changed. My love for you hasn't, I want to make you happy, because I also know that you already make me happy."

Celia was moved by his words, a patient man that accepted her the way she was. She did not have to think about it anymore, it wasn't awkward either; she hugged and kissed him and cried "Yes, I want to marry you!" He kept his forehead pressed onto hers, he smiled in between tears of joy and took out a small box with a delicate ring. "I bought a new one in case the Tiffany's was jinxed." He put it on her left finger and kissed her hand, she couldn't stop smiling.

"I love it, thank you and I love you. It wasn't anything wrong with the ring, the time wasn't right then. I was unsure of a lot of things but now, I'm certain of everything. I want to be with you." She said and they kissed again.

They walked home, he squeezed her hand tightly just to know that it was real, he asked her "So, when do you want to get married and where? Are you still no church wedding?"

She thought for a moment, when she married Joe, they married at city hall and now she wasn't a divorcee, she was a widow.

"Maybe we could get married at church if you want. For me it's all the same since God is everywhere, so if you want, we can do it." David smiled big; it seems like it was his dreams to marry in a church. He had never been married before, so she would be his first official wife.

"Then I want to tell you that I know which church we should choose: St Michael's catholic church." He said, with tears in his eyes. Celia stopped to hug him "Hey, sure, if this is the one you have your heart set on then this is the one. Why so sad?"

David sniffed, explaining "My parents, well my adoptive ones, married here. So now I want to do the same, they were happy, and I want the same for us." She smiled, took his hand tighter and whispered, "I think we should go home, I'm going to cheer you up the way you like." He blushed, she was so untethered now, he liked this side of her: they got home quickly, and it was like they fused together into one.

"Wow, that was a wake-up call and a happy one. Think we could have some ice-cream?" he said while she was curling up in his arms. It was a cold evening, around 10 pm but still ice-cream sounded like a great idea. He went up, put on his boxers, and went to the fridge, found some chocolate and a lemon sorbet. He brought both boxes and 2 spoons. They sat up on the bed, Celia with her bra and underwear on and David with his boxers, she wrapped the sheets around her back, but he moved so he could sit behind her, to warm her up.

She smiled as she put the spoon with chocolate ice-cream in her mouth, a silent mm was heard, and David took one bite of the lemon. "This is life, to be here with you, in this bed. I thought I would end up alone, after I lost you. I hated myself for that, you have no idea." He said, moved his cheek closer to hers.

Celia thought for a while, she remembered how tough it was for her when she heard him say that he loved Tamara. She stroked his face and said "Don't think about that anymore, we're together and we're getting married. Give me some of that." He gave her the spoon with lemon ice-cream, she took it and spill it on his bare chest. David winced and she turned to face him "I think I like this taste better with lemon." She licked the ice-cream off him and he couldn't sit still any longer, he put the buckets on the floor and pulled her down towards the foot end of the bed. They laughed when they realized how funny it looked, he kissed her neck and proceeded to her belly. Celia was ecstatic, she laughed and moaned. He moved back to her face, they kissed, and he entered her carefully, grabbing her buttocks.

Celia got out of bed, David still asleep, she picked up the melted ice-cream cartons and threw them into the trash. Her neck was sore, she went to the bathroom and looked, he left 2 big hickeys on either side, she nodded her head to herself and washed her face.

Then she noticed her swollen lips, he surely did a number on her, she thought to herself and smiled big. She stood by the door, watched him sleep. It was only 7 am on a Saturday morning, she should let him be for a few hours but last night had been such an exquisite moment that she felt she wanted more.

"How on earth did someone who barely had any interest in sex suddenly become sex-goddess number 1?" she thought to herself, maybe it was the lack of sex in her youth? She didn't become active until she began her relationship with David all those years ago.

Celia was still up in her thoughts when David woke up and saw her standing in the doorway in her robe. "What are you doing over there? Come here, you." She went over to the bed and threw herself into his arms, he purred in her ear "Mm good morning babe, how did you sleep?" She responded just as eagerly "Very good sir, and you?" They shared a passionate kiss; she moved her hand closer to his groin and felt that the passionate kiss was an understatement. "Well sir, I believe we were thinking the same thing. Shall we pick up where we left off?" she said cheekily, and he shut her up with a kiss.

CHAPTER 23:
CHURCH WEDDING

Celia looked at herself in the mirror, her mother in tears from the side and her sister sitting right behind. "You look like an angel, I'm so glad you decided for a white dress." said her mother and wiped her tears. It's true, she looked like an angel. She always thought that to marry someone she needed to be a virgin to be able to dress in white. Now she knew that it wasn't necessary.

"I think I'm ready, is he in there?" Celia said, nervous and almost ready to cry. Her sister handed over something blue: a hairpin with blue stones. "This is your something blue and borrowed, no rush to return it." She smiled, gave her sister a hug and put the pin in the hair. "My turn. Here's your something new, from your dad and me." Celia's mother handed over a little box, it was a Swarovski box with a pair of earrings in silver. Maritime theme, something her mother absolutely loved. "Thank you, mom, tell dad thanks too. Is he?" she said and put them on. "He's with David, I think he's extremely nervous. I heard him talk on and on, so yeah, he's there. Ready?"

They walked out first, letting Celia walk out alone. By the entrance she met her stepdad Fred and he admired her "You look beautiful, just as the last time my dear. I hope to God, that you get to be that happy again. Know that Joe is up there, celebrating in your honor."

She was crying now, Thank God for waterproof make-up. They walked calmly to the altar where David and the minister was waiting. He took a deep breath, couldn't help but shed a few tears to see his bride looking like an angel.

"You look heaven sent." He said and gave her a quick kiss on the cheek through her veil. They kneeled before the minister, he spoke some words in Latin and everyone sat down.

While he spoke about the sacrament that is to be married, David kept his eyes on her, whispered suddenly "I can't believe you're here with me. I'm so happy." She smiled but didn't want to look too much, she whispered back "I love you, there's no other place I'd rather be."

In the front row was her mother, stepdad, sister, her husband and kids and Ally, David's daughter. There were other people there but no one as important as her family, the ones that genuinely cared for her.

"David Eugene Castle, do you take Celia Andrea Caceres to be your lawfully wedded wife, to have and to hold in sickness and in health until death do you part?" said the minister loud and clear. He looked happy at Celia and said "Yes, I do." Putting the wedding band that had been handed over by Celia's dad.

"Celia Andrea Caceres, do you take David Eugene Castle to be your lawfully wedded husband to have and to hold in sickness and in health until death do you part?" She turned to Ally, that handed over the ring and put it on his finger: "I do."

They smiled towards each other and held hands until the minister said "By the power invested in me by

God and the catholic church of St Michael's I now pronounce you husband and wife. You may now kiss the bride."

David lifted the veil over her face to kiss her, he saw some tears in her eyes. But he realized that it was of happiness. "I love you." He kissed her carefully and she smiled "Love you too."

They walked out from the church to meet the small crowd of people outside to greet them. David had a car by one side that he was going to drive to their honeymoon, a hotel in Northampton. They couldn't be away too long since they both worked. It was a blue Camaro, with white letters that said "Just Married" in Cezanne handwriting. Celia stopped to read, she remembered what Joe had said in the letter: I'll be there.

She threw her bouquet to the crowd, got into the car and they drove off. "How did you know?" she said quietly and took David's hand, while he held the wheel with the other one. "Because he told me to, I know how much this means to you and you know that I'd do anything for you."

About an hour driving they reached Northampton before nightfall, her dress wasn't all big and flashy so she could get out of the car without any problems. He parked inside and they took their overnight bags to the reception "Reservation for Mr. and Mrs. Castle please." he said to the concierge, putting his arm around Celia's waist. The concierge found their reservation, gave them the room key, and told them that complimentary champagne and strawberries were coming in a few minutes.

They took the elevator to the 7th floor, opened room 741 and it was huge. The honeymoon suite was an apartment with a big bed, tv, shower, bathroom, closets, and table. David scooped his wife up in his arms and carried her to the bed, she giggled, and he removed his tie. She had already removed her veil when they got in the car but was thinking about getting out of the dress, then she remembered that the champagne was on it's way. "I got you something, here, open it." He said and handed over a big thin box that said "La Perla" on it, she blushed and opened it. There was a beautiful black set of lingerie, expensive one because she had only heard of "La Perla" in a movie.

"It's beautiful, thank you honey. Want me to try it on?" she said seductively, and he leaned in to kiss her. "Sure, but wait until the waiter leaves the champagne otherwise, he's in for a very nice surprise." he was laughing now. "Tease." She winked at him, her husband.

The champagne arrived, Celia had not drunk alcoholic beverage and maybe it was a good reason. A glass later, she was drunk for the first time in her life. When he tried to help her to their bed, she whispered "So Mr. Castle, how do you want your wife tonight? Want me to try on the fancy lingerie?"

He smiled at her, helped her off her wedding dress and got a pajama shirt from her suitcase. He took off her bra to put on the shirt, but she kept moving her arms and he said "As beautiful you are naked miss, I'm not going to take advantage of my wife. Besides, making love we can do any day. Drunk? No, not on my watch." She pulled his shirt to kiss him, he answered carefully as he felt that he was aroused to see his wife half naked. It would seem like she noticed as she began unbuttoning his pants too, he held her hand softly, but she moved it towards her naked chest. David sighed as he felt her bare skin with his hand, he bent to kiss her, and she pulled him closer to kiss her neck. He breathed heavy and he lifted her up, she ripped apart his shirt and he threw it on the floor. They kissed, grunted their way towards one of the closest walls and she held onto his neck while he searched underneath her dress to remove her underwear. Celia giggled, until she felt him enter her, they exchanged kisses, moaned and he moved her back to the bed.

David touched her bare skin, the tiny hairs in the back of her neck raised to his touch and he kissed it. She was snoring next him, face down in the bed. He put the blanket on her back so she wouldn't be cold and turned on the tv, found a music channel, left it on.

CHAPTER 24:
WORK, WORK, WORK

It had been a year since they married and now, they were focused on working: Celia was doing lectures in different universities and David was doing research for the hospital. Still, they made time for each other since their love hardly turned down. It was like making love was breathing for them, something not quite common in other relationships.

She was gathering her things in the assembly hall, when she received a phone call from her husband "Hello there Mr. Castle, how are you doing?" He chuckled in the phone "Hey there, I'm looking for this really hot lecturer that was supposed to talk about something. I don't really care what she was going to discuss but her legs…oh my God." They laughed, he wanted to pick her up at the university and she said that in about 45 minutes she would be out the door. "See you in the parking lot then baby, love you, bye."

She went to the teachers' lounge to put some of her books in her locker and pick up her jacket when one of the teachers, Hunter James approached her. "Hey Celia, how was class?" For a moment she thought she was alone but wasn't at all bothered by him. She knew he was the universities "dog" and since she was happily married, she resisted his supposed charms. "Hey Hunter, not bad at all. They're not angels but hey, they listen. I need to schedule an exam in 2 weeks, do I need to talk it over with some other teacher or do I do it myself?" He came closer, she could smell his cheap aftershave, that almost was cheesy rather than refreshing. "You know, you're the only one that hasn't fallen in my charms and I'm wondering why."

Celia was disgusted by his comment, but if he tried anything, she was an experienced Aikido student. Something Joe, her late husband had convinced her to take classes for any reason: exercise, self-defense or even to master self-preservation.

"Hunter, you're crossing a line. If you continue, I'll have to report you to the school board." She said, keychain in her fingers in case it went sideways. "Come on, that boring husband of yours couldn't possibly keep you satisfied. No one is going to see us here, there's no one around." He continued, Celia knew that if she hit him, they could report her to the board. She moved away slowly and picked up an umbrella to defend herself, he moved closer, and she hit him twice with it. "You try that again, I'll have no leniency with you!" He put up his hands, as in "I surrender".

She walked out to see David standing in the parking lot, she ran over to him and said, "A male colleague just tried to seduce me." He looked mad and wanted to go inside to kick his ass, but she stopped him "No, no honey, I'm okay. I'm going to report him though, no other female teacher should go through this." She took out her phone and called the director who suggested to also call the police. David drove away while she was on the phone, still mad. As she finished her conversation, she saw his tense jaw "Hey, I'm okay, it's been dealt with. Come on, let's stop for a while."

They stopped close to a wooden area, in Vale Village, got out of the car and he found a closed-up area with a lot of trees.

He began kissing her, she didn't mind but when he tried to undress her, she asked, "Uh baby, are you okay?" and stopped him. David was frustrated, still pretty much upset what Celia had been through with the colleague. "What? You don't want to have sex outside? Or was it just something you did with Joe?" She looked at him with big eyes, he had never been rude to her "No, we never had sex outside. It would've been our thing, you and me if we were doing it for the right reason not for a stupidity." She adjusted her blazer and went back to the car, took out her bag and walked away. A few meters away there was a bus stop towards town which she took, tears were running down her cheeks.

Her phone rang a few times, she didn't want to pick up: 10 missed calls, 3 voicemails and 1 text message from David. She read the text only: "Baby, I'm sorry, I'm so sorry. Please, please pick up or call me back. Don't leave." She didn't reply, went instead to Prêt a Manger to buy noodle salad for the evening and some fruit. When she got home, David wasn't there so she went to take a shower quickly. It was a first fight, they had disagreements before but never fought like this. Celia cried in the shower, got out and wrapped herself in a towel. She ate the noodle salad directly from the carton, had some fruit and went to bed, leaving one of the containers with salad and fruit to David, with a note: Eat this.

It was quiet in the apartment, so she fell asleep. Later in the evening she heard noise in the kitchen, lights in the living room and a quiet walking to the bed.

He got under the covers and turned off the reading lamp, she carefully turned over and he was laying on his side, a quiet sniff could be heard from him.

She got up from bed and went to the kitchen, he had eaten the noodle salad and the fruit, there was a note on the counter: Thank you honey. Celia smiled, went back to bed, and wrapped her arms around his waist. She felt his hands on hers and he whispered "I'm sorry, it was stupid what I said and I didn't mean it."

He turned over to face her and to his surprise, she was naked. Within seconds he removed his t-shirt and his pajama pants, wrapped his body around her, kissed her and in between kisses wanted to say something but she didn't let him. She climbed on top of him, and he moved his hand towards her face, caressed it.

The sun shined through the slightly opened window, onto her bare back. David was awake, looking at her sleeping. "Hey, you, okay?" she said, and he leaned in to kiss her "Yes, thank you. I'm sorry baby, my behavior yesterday was terrible and I'm sorry you had to take the bus home. Still, you managed to buy food for me, even though I was such an ass."

She shut him up with a kiss and he turned her down onto the bed, his kisses moved from her mouth to her collarbone, down her chest, to her belly and then back to her mouth. Celia moaned, their breath became faster and she suddenly gasped.

"You know, we should try the outside thing, but in a tent. Can't have people or animals watching." She said and he laughed towards her neck.

Sunday, the whole weekend had already passed and Celia didn't want to go back to work the following morning. David was making pancakes in the kitchen while she was watching tv, but she couldn't keep still anymore.

She went to the kitchen and said, "Do you have many left?" He smiled and said "I'm making 2 batches, so we have some dessert for the week. Why, do you need something done?" She kissed him, he kissed her back and she pulled his arms towards her. "Ha-ha no, no I can't leave this here. I still have about 30 pancakes left to fry babe." She turned off the heat and pulled him to the bedroom. They laughed in between, he pulled her up in his arms and continued to their bed.

"Will you continue to fry the pancakes now or should I just give it up?" Celia, wrapping herself in a sheet. David was sitting on her side, bare chested. Since he didn't respond anything, she moved closer and put her hands around his waist "Hey, are you okay? So silent." He stroked her hands, moved them up to his face to kiss them, he sighed "No baby, I'm fine, it's just that for a moment I felt like I had lost you again. Over a stupid comment, I should've just thought about it."

She moved even closer to him, wrapped her legs around his waist and held on to his chest to hear him breath shakily "Hey, it's part of being married you know. It can't always be perfect, but I know that love always conquers all, even silly comments. And I mean silly as in the best sense of the word, because if you want us to have sex outside in nature well yes, we can. I don't want to it to be because some jackass tried to seduce me, he couldn't be more wrong because I love you, I don't care about others."

David listened to his clever wife, he kissed her arms again and moved facing her. She climbed onto his legs, and he removed the sheets "I'll deal with the pancakes, right now, I just want you." Celia giggled in his ear.

CHAPTER 25:
THE LOST SONG

Celia and David were dancing to a slow song in their apartment, after a long day at work. It's something they did often because she had always dreamed that she would dance with her future husband.

Suddenly another song came on, she didn't recognize it but the voice sounded familiar "Who's that? I know that voice." He smiled and kept her close, but she went to check the playlist, to her surprise and admiration, she saw that it was David who sang. "It's you, you're singing. But you never told me this!"

David stopped the playlist, explaining "It was when you left me, I have this friend that works in a record company, and he helped me "record" my pain. It was only that time and no, I'm not going to make an album. Come on, let's dance." He pulled her arm towards him; she stayed in his arms and kissed his neck.

She was making dinner and David came in from the living room, humming a tune, they smiled towards each other and then he moved in behind her to hum in her ear. "You could set the table, while I finish this honey. Don't forget the napkins." She said and continued stirring, it would seem like David wasn't at all interested in doing anything. He lowered the heat on the stove and turned her around, kissed her carefully. "I might as well put this on low heat." She said and turned the kitchen knob on low, to continue kissing David all the way to the bedroom.

He chuckled under his breath, he took off his white t-shirt as he grabbed Celia from the waist "Aren't you the feisty one, come here you." They kissed, more intense now, she was about to take off her t-shirt when he said, quietly "No, let me do it." She smiled and he took it off her, slowly, caressing her shoulders, her waist and pulled her close to kiss her.

The bed got into a mess, pillows on the floor and both wrapped in a sheet, Celia blushing and David, trying to keep from blushing as well. "Well, think dinner is ready or ruined?" she finally said to him, he smiled but wasn't facing her. She got out of bed to check, dinner wasn't ruined so she turned off the heat, put the lid on and put the pot to the side. He was laying back on the bed, sheet covering his private area and his legs were outside the covers. She took off her wrapping and removed his as well, he laughed but got up on the bed to bring her down. They kissed, he grabbed her buttocks to her surprised staring, and she leaned in to kiss him again. She forced him down on the bed, kissing him even more intense, there was need in her way of kissing him. He took a deep breath, moved away a lock of hair from her face, looked deep into her eyes and said, "I love you so much Celia." She smiled, kissed his eyelids, cheeks, and nose before grabbing his chin to kiss him.

They rested in bed; it had been an hour approximately when David was humming again. It wasn't the song, this was another one.

"Sing it to me." She said and looked at him, he smiled and whispered "No, I'm too bad at singing to sing like this." Celia insisted "Please honey, sing it to me." He sighed, kissed her head, and began: It was sweet, corny and he had a great singing voice.

She closed her eyes, it was like being married to the Phantom of the opera, she tapped with her fingers on his chest, and he smiled as he tried to continue singing. Celia must have fallen asleep, because when she woke up, he was gone. He left her a note: "Sleep my sweetheart, I'm going to the supermarket for dinner. Be right back. Love you!"

She got out of bed, took a shower, and got dressed. Since it was a little cold, she made some tea and sat in the couch, when David came home. "Hey, bought some dinner. Want some Korean BBQ?" he said and put the bags on the floor. Celia walked over and gave him a kiss, took the bags to the kitchen. He was washing his hands when she sneaked up behind him and said "Mm…you smell so good, even better than the food." He turned around to kiss her, sniffed her neck and said "You smell good, I think we should leave the food in the fridge and just go back to bed. What do you think?"

She smiled, hugged him and said "You know, lately, all we do is have sex, oh and eat of course. How come we are like this? It's like we're obsessed!" Now Celia was concerned, according to her friends, some have sex for a whole year and then they kind of get tired of each other.

But not them, more than once a week, every week. David sat down in the couch, with Celia on his lap, she was stroking his hair. He said "Maybe other people don't love each other that much, I love you too much to let you go pretty much anywhere. I lost you for a long time and I'm not going to waste any time." He stroked her arm with his nose, and she got up, he was confused but then he saw that she was crying. "Hey, why are you crying?" He went up to hug her and brought her back to the couch, she sniffed "It's so beautiful, what you just said. I love you too and yes, lately we've been overly active and it's because we love each other. It's not for pleasure only, right?" He chuckled in her ear "Of course it is, you're the hottest woman on the Planet and I wouldn't have it any other way babe." He tickled her and she put her head on his neck, he patted her butt and said "Now, let's go have some Korean food and then do something fun, want to see a movie?"

They went out to the theater nearby to see a movie and took a walk after. "It was a good movie; I love Fast and the Furious." She said and squeezed his hand, he smiled "That's because you like Vin Diesel or that other guy, his character, Han." "Yeah, I like them both but only because they're genuine sweet guys, well hot too but I don't know, you're hot and I love you more." She smiled, he wrapped his arms around her and said, "I know, come on let's go home and have some hot tea."

Another day at the office, Celia was tired. It was only 2:30 and still she needed to have one last meeting at 4 before she could go home, David was also at work, and they had exchanged sweet messages throughout the day.

She looked out the window, soon it was time for Christmas, and she had no idea what to give David. He never said he needed anything, she had checked his wardrobe, maybe a new shirt since she tended to rip them apart when they made love. A new perfume would be nice, something masculine that takes out his comforting smell of home.

"Celia? Your 4 o'clock is here." Said the receptionist and she woke up from her thoughts, gave her a smile and nodded to send the person in. It was Ally, with a big smile, standing at the door "Hey mom, how are you?" They hugged, sat down in the sofa, and talked for a while. She asked how her mom Tamara was doing "How's your mother?" Ally took a deep breath, took Celia's hand and said "My mother passed, 2 days ago. I got the news today from her caretaker and well the funeral is next week. I was kind of hoping you and dad could accompany me, he doesn't know yet."

Even though Ally didn't have a good relationship with her mother, she still felt pain for her loss, Celia hugged her and said "Of course honey, you're still my loving daughter and I'll be happy to go, with your father of course. I'm sorry for your loss, would you like to stay at our place?" She nodded, since they had a spare room, she could fix it with the bed sofa and linen.

"Anna, could you clear my schedule please? I'm going home with my daughter, see you tomorrow. Thanks." She told the receptionist through the intercom.

"It feels bigger than last time I was here, thank you, for letting me stay with you guys." Ally said, helping Celia while making the bed. "Of course, honey, you need to be around family now, do you need help with anything else regarding funeral arraignments?" she said and fluffed the pillows, Ally looked out the window and responded "Well, I took care of it. She wanted to be cremated and there's this little cemetery where her relatives are buried. The apartment is for sale already, she did that herself and well the stuff inside, I don't want anything. It could go to charity, some of the money are for bills and the rest is to me but I think that I should give some to you for you know, stuff." Celia came over to her, hugged her and said "No need honey, you're my daughter, besides I have no need of extra money. My late husband, Joe, left me quite an estate and I'll be more than happy to give you to anything you might need."

"Baby I'm home, hey you have the same shoes as Ally. Where did… hey honey, good to see you!" David said from the door as soon as he saw Ally. They hugged and she broke the news for him, he took a deep breath and hugged her again "I'm sorry honey, so very sorry. I hope your mother found peace in the end, how are you holding up?" Ally explained what she had told Celia, they sat down for a while, when she was in the kitchen making a snack. "Here we go sweethearts, Ally, do you want some iced tea or a soda?" she said and brought it to the living room.

"Thanks mom, iced tea will be just great. Oh yum, I forgot to have lunch today." Ally said and took one of the sandwiches, Celia looked concerned "Want some dinner instead? We can order take-out." Ally nodded "No thanks mom, to have a snack with you and then I really just want to sleep."

They talked for a while and Ally went to bed early, so David and Celia sat alone for a few hours, watching something on tv. He began caressing her neck, she moved closer to his side and tapped him on his chest. He sniffed her hair, suddenly stroking her back, going lower and lower until he reached her butt. She moved her hand inside his shirt, felt his skin underneath her hand and he shivered. He turned his face to kiss her, she kissed him back and he whispered, "You think she might hear us?" She smiled, "No she's in the room by the kitchen and ours is close to the entrance door." He grabbed her hand and ran into their bedroom, locking the door behind him. Celia sat on the bed and looked at him with desire, she began unbuttoning her blouse and he stopped her "No, let me, by the way, are you too fond of this blouse?" She laughed a little and went to her closet, there was a bunch of them hanging in different colors "Not really, it's a uniform. Why?" He moved her closer to the bed and opened the buttons one by one, she took a deep breath, it was difficult to stay in place. They kissed, he grabbed her waist and pulled her up in his arms. Her bare skin felt hot underneath his hand and he moved to sit down with her, he was still wearing a t-shirt, so she removed it.

He held her close for a while, felt her skin underneath his touch as he removed her black bra. David placed her on the bed, laid his hand on her chest, touching her carefully, arousing her entire being. He kissed her neck, collarbone, moved to her pale breasts and down to her belly, he drew his fingers along the middle of her chest like he was drawing a picture. Celia smiled, she pulled him into an embrace, and they kissed passionately.

It was almost 5:30 am, Celia was asleep with David and Ally was getting ready for work. She was working as an assistant nurse in a hospital and had her morning shift. She made them coffee and tea, left a note on the table saying "Dear mom and dad, thank you so much for letting me stay during this difficult time. I'll see you later, making dinner tonight so don't bring anything. Love you both, love Ally."

She quietly closed the door and locked, Celia had given her a pair of keys so she could come and go as she pleased. But she knew she needed to stay in her own apartment after the funeral, but right now she really needed some company.

Celia got up, it was almost 8 am and today she didn't need to go to work, she took a glimpse at David who snored away and smiled. She went to the bathroom to take a shower and she heard someone at the door, David was standing there in his boxers "Care to shower together honey?" he said and grabbed her waist, she giggled and turned on the shower.

She took off her silky nightgown, threw it on top of the washing machine and David stared at her "You're one fine woman Celia, I don't think I could ever stop loving you." They kissed under the water, he stroked her wet hair out of her face, laughing.

They were both drying themselves, David was in his boxers now and took his towel to dry her back. He looked at her through the mirror, she met his gaze and smiled, turned around to kiss him. "You know, we should really do something else. All we do is work and sleep together, it can't be healthy, can it?" she said in between kisses, he took a deep breath, almost like absorbing her soul.

David let her go for a moment and stared into her eyes, she couldn't help but smile and he scooped her up in his arms carrying her to the bedroom, gently putting her on the bed. "David, what are we doing here?" she said, and he shut her up with kisses, then said "Well Mrs. Castle, I'm going to have sex with you and hope you want it too." She laughed and nodded her head, grabbed his neck to pull him closer, he reached her collarbone, nibbled her ear carefully and removed her towel to kiss her chest.

Celia could barely breath, when he entered her, and they moved in sync until reaching climax. "Wow, that was…" hc said, laid next to her and she moved to his chest, kissed it "Exquisite, we're getting better at this."

CHAPTER 26: REACHING THE STARS

It was a dark afternoon, raining all day and Celia was stuck at the office with some paperwork, phone calls and emails. David had texted her if she wanted to get some dinner but had to decline since she had way too much work in hands.

He went to get take-out, some Korean BBQ since it was her favorite and had invited Ally to join them, she had some important news to share. Lately, after the funeral she had been very quiet, probably missing her mother but he was eager to cheer up his daughter. He had also contacted the receptionist on Celia's floor and asked her to facilitate an office where they could have dinner. She was more than happy to help. When he arrived, he asked "Hey, is the room ready?" "Yes Mr. Castle, she's in a phone meeting right now but I'll make sure to meet you there, 45 minutes good for you?" "Yeah, I'm just waiting for my daughter and then we're good to go." He said and went to the kitchen, put the dinner in the oven on low heat to keep it warm and waited for Ally in the entrance.

"Hey dad, how are you? Where's mom?" Ally said and gave him a hug, he told her that she was still working and that they were surprising her there. They sneaked into the office, directly to the kitchen and then to the empty office they were having dinner in. "She's coming, hide." He said and they hid behind the table, Celia walked in and said to the receptionist "The meeting is here? But it's dark and no one is here, where's the light button?" she turned it on, and they jumped out from behind the table "Surprise!!"

Celia jumped backwards, frightened but then very happy to see them both "What on Earth? What are you doing here? Hey honey, how are you? Baby, I thought you went home."

David gave her a hug "No, I called Ally to join me here, since you couldn't go home to have dinner, we brought it to you. You have to eat, what better than to have a family dinner." Celia was happy, she pulled them both towards her to hug them. She said "David, maybe we could invite the receptionist Amy to join us." And David said "No need, I offered dinner and she took it with her. Her boyfriend works downstairs as a janitor, so they'll have a good company."

They all washed their hands, sat down to eat. David pinched Celia on her thigh, Ally was sitting on the other side so she didn't notice. "So, honey, how's work?" said Celia and took a bite, David looked like he wanted to say something but kept quiet, he already knew what Ally wanted to tell them "Well it's great, but it's not the reason why I'm here today. I'm moving to Canada with my boyfriend and I wanted you to know. He got a job there and I want to go with him."

Celia was surprised, they had been dating for a while, but she never thought that she would move "Oh honey, that's a long road ahead. Are you sure?" Ally smiled big, she was a grown up now and she also knew when she moved to the US that she took the decision on her own.

Celia took her glass and raised it "Well then, as long as you do this for you and what you want in life, cheers honey.

We'll support you in anything you need because we love you." She was moved by the support and happy, because she was going to live with the man of her dreams.

After dinner, Celia needed to finish some work and told her husband plus daughter to go home, she would be home in few hours. "Alright mom, we'll talk soon, take care." Ally said and gave her a hug, Celia whispered "I'm very happy for you to follow your heart honey, keep me posted." She gave David a kiss and said "I'll be home soon, see you then."

They left, happy. David gave his daughter a ride home and he stopped by a convenience store to buy some last-minute snacks. Unknown number called him "Castle. Yeah, sure, what's it about? Huh, now? No sorry, can't tonight. Tomorrow morning, yeah, great. Thanks, bye." It was work related, so he would tell Celia when she got home.

At their home, he lit some electric candles and placed the snacks on the table. He took a quick shower and changed to his boxers and his robe, checked the time and according to what she had said, she would be home in an hour. Watched a little tv, had some snacks and was nodding off a bit.

Celia came home, saw the candles, and sneaked in but David was very much asleep on the sofa with his robe and the tv on low volume. She smiled, grabbed a blanket, and put it carefully on him. He did look very inviting, but she was also very tired, took a shower and laid down in the other side of the sofa.

"Babe, I didn't hear you come home. I'm so sorry to have fallen asleep, come here." He said at 5:30 in the morning, Celia was comfortable in her side but moved to his. He held on to her, kissed her cheek and they went back to sleep.

"Good morning sunshine, time to get up." A voice whispered in her ear, the sun was shining directly in her eyes and then she saw a smile that she recognized "Joe?" The voice, suddenly had a face and it was her late husband, sitting right there by her side. "Hey honey, I'm back and here with you. How are things?"

She hugged him; it was so unreal to see him again. They talked a little, he was happy that she had found happiness again. "I miss you, every day." He disappeared and she sat up in the sofa, the sun wasn't shining anymore, David was there, still asleep. She looked out the window, saw a little ray of sunshine fading away in the clouds. It was about to rain, but she stood there and let her tears fall. "I love you, always." She whispered and felt a pair of hands holding her waist, David had wakened up. "Hey, who are you talking to?" He kissed her cheek, felt the salt in her tears and she said, "I got a visit from Joe in my dream, he's happy to see us together." David looked out the window, he smiled and said "It's thanks to him, if he wouldn't have written that letter to me, I wouldn't have pursued you. I was far too ashamed to even talk to you but then he gave me his blessing, because he understood how much I still loved you even though I was such an ass. I owe him my happiness with you."

He took her hand and turned her over, hugged her tightly and she said "He cared for both of us, well you in his way and me well he told me. Thank you, Joe, for giving me a great man to love after you."

David looked into her eyes, took her face in his hands, and kissed her gently "I think that it's time for some breakfast maybe, what do you say?" She purred, nodding and went to get the teapot. They had breakfast on the balcony, it was nice and calm, occasional lusty exchange of winks until he suddenly got up "I can't wait until we finish, come on." Celia looked confused but went with him to the bedroom, the lusty glances was more than that. He kissed her with intense passion, she could barely take a breath, removed her robe and there she was, naked and at his disposition. His lips moved towards her pale skin, to her neck, down to her breasts and back to her lips. She laughed a little, apparently her neck was getting ticklish nowadays, he laid her down on the bed and laid beside her. He pulled up the covers so she wouldn't freeze but lifted them up, placed his hand on her belly to "walk" with his fingers up and down. She placed her hand on his chin, felt his jawline with the tip of her finger and stopped at his lips, drawing on them. David kissed her finger and moved on top of her, he laid down trying not to hurt her, but she was more than willing to hold on to him. He kept his nose on top of hers, nuzzling her with a smile and carefully entered her. Those lusty glances by the table had been changed for pure love, she could tell that he truly loved her. David helped her overcome her sadness of losing her husband and maybe she always kept a piece of him in her heart, like a security blanket.

CHAPTER 27:
PAST, PRESENT, FUTURE

It was date night and David was already late, it had been a long day at the office. He texted Celia a quick "I'm running late baby, wait for me in the office, don't go anywhere." But one last phone call took more time than needed, the girl from the flower shop had called. He found it odd since he ordered flowers a long time ago and now, she was calling, maybe she just wanted to sell him more flowers. "David, yeah, hey, of course I remember. Now? No, I'm sorry I can't. Thank you, but I have a wife you know, heh no problem. Thank you, you too. Bye."

He nodded to himself, before Celia he wasn't a popular man among women. Not even in school, he was thin looking with no muscles and girls back then liked the guys with big guns almost like Arnold Schwarzenegger. Now he was normal size, not that many muscles but strong and Celia had never commented on his arms other than she liked him completely. He would make sure to ask her when they meet up to drive home.

Celia was walking through the park, close to his office. She had never been afraid to walk alone in the dark, since she was very independent, she never asked anyone to walk her home. Besides, David would be happy to meet her so close by instead of having to pick her up. There was noise behind her, she tried to keep a calm pace, but it seemed like the person was matching hers.

As she was turning to the street where David's office was someone grabbed her arm and threw her into the ground. A man, by the size, grabbed her bag and tried to take it from her. She kicked him in the balls and tried to get away, but he got a hold on her, hit her over the face and she fell on the ground. She got up fast and got a few punches in, but he was too strong, this time he threw her in the ground, and she hit her head on the ground, loosing conscience.

A guy with his dog found her and called police and ambulance. David was notified that she was in the hospital with severe head trauma, a broken wrist, and possible broken ribs. He was in the hospital within minutes and spoke to the doctor "Doctor, how is she?". The doctor, a young man in his 30s looking very serious at the x-rays taken of her injuries "Mr. Castle, your wife suffered some serious trauma. Right now, she's in surgery regarding a small bleeding into her brain. It will take hours until we know the severity of her injuries. I'm sorry but we must wait."

He sat down, not knowing what he could do to help her. Despair got the best of him, and he cried, praying that she would pull through.

In surgery, Celia was in deep sleep. She saw light on a green field, it was warm out, she was barefoot.

A voice on the other side of the field spoke to her, she recognized it, in fact, she would know that voice anywhere: Joe. She ran to him, he walked towards her, and they met in the middle, hugging.

"Hey honey, I've missed you so much! Come on, let's sit." He showed her to a tree filled with fruit, she sat down, and he sat next to her, holding on to her. "Where are we?" she rested onto his chest, he was wearing a black Hawaiian shirt and linen pants. His hair was just the way he wore it and he smelled just as when they were married.

"This is paradise, or some people call it Eden, depending on how you see it. For me, it's just perfection since you're here now. I know what happened to you, but I'm divided on whether you should stay with me and live happily ever after or go back to David and continue your life together." He said and kissed her on the cheek, she felt at home with him, maybe it wasn't so bad to stay, besides she didn't even know who David was.

"Who's David and why can't I just stay here? You're the man I want in my life, I don't need anyone else." She said and cuddled up, he held his hand on hers and whispered, "You have a family, what about them?"

Celia didn't want to think, the sunlight kept hitting her eyes and she felt like she couldn't continue sitting in the shadows of the tree. She heard a noise, a voice that whispered things "BP is dropping, give her 5 mg of Epi, start contractions, charge 200, clear.

Try again, 10 mg of Epi, contractions, we're losing her. Charge 360, clear." Joe was fading away, he held her hand and said, "Go now honey, one day we'll meet again." He let her go, she was back on the operating table and her blood pressure was normal again.

Celia woke up in a big room, sunlight entering through a small spring in the curtains, she had a needle in her arm connected to a bag of drip and respiratory tube in her mouth. A man was sleeping by her side, she didn't recognize him but she couldn't dare to wake him up. She rang the help clock by her bed and the nurse came, she looked so happy and brought the cart to remove the tubes. Celia felt like she was about to vomit but could contain herself, the man asleep by her bed woke up. His kind eyes looked tired; had he been sleeping here all night?

"Hey baby, how are you feeling? Are you in pain?" he said and kissed her forehead, his voice was new, she hadn't heard it before but the kiss was somehow well known. "Who are you?" she said quietly and opened her big brown eyes. The man looked surprised but didn't want to make her upset, he smiled weakly and went out to see the doctor. He was filing some reports and saw David looking distressed "Hey, Mr. Castle. Your wife is doing very well after her surgery, the swelling is completely gone, and she could be out in a few weeks." He smiled to the doctor, but his concern was more like why she didn't recognize him. The doctor found it weird and walked with him to her room "Hi Celia, how are you feeling?"

She smiled and sat up "I'm doing fine doctor, I think I'm recovering very well but I'm sorry to say, is this your colleague?" He looked concerned, did some random checks and then explained "No, this is your husband, David. He's been here, guarding you all this time to keep you safe." She nodded, to David's surprise she responded "I'm sorry but I don't know anyone named David, my husbands name is Joe. Is he here?" The doctor and David looked at each other with surprise, before telling her that he could walk in any minute.

Outside David and the doctor spoke about her lack of memory, it could be temporarily after the operation and work out in the end. "She will be under surveillance, I'll talk to a counselor to book some sessions for her. If that doesn't help, then we would need to reevaluate." David felt tears coming, he couldn't bear to lose his wife again. He went back to her room, to look at her through the window, she was asleep again. He thought to himself, wishing he could be there to hug and comfort her, instead he was standing in the doorway.

It had been 2 weeks since she woke up, not knowing who David was. She had been up and doing exercises, memory check and still nothing. The counselor meetings had not been very giving, she knew who she was, remembered her family and her husband but not David as him but the man that died so many years ago. The doctor decided to let her go home but she would have to stay in David's and her apartment, without David. He checked into a hotel but told her that he would check in on her until her husband came back from his trip overseas.

Celia was grateful to the kind stranger that would keep tabs on her but still wanted to talk to her husband, so David tried to imitate his voice through the payphone down the street. He called her home and she remembered Joe's voice "Hello?" "Uh, hi Celia, it's me, Joe. How are you feeling honey?" She was thrilled to hear him again, they talked for a while about the accident and when he would come home. "I can't yet, I'm stuck in the US but as soon as I can I'll be home. I love you Celia, so, so much. I'll call you next week, okay? I miss you." He heard her endearments and hung up; his heart broke into thousands of pieces.

Another 2 weeks, he called every week to see how she was, and she kept asking the same questions: When he was coming home to her. David couldn't keep it together and told her that he was coming home that same evening. She was ecstatic, found the most gorgeous clothes in her wardrobe and waited for him to come home. He had asked her to turn down the lights, he had some irritation on his eyes and couldn't stand it so she just left a few candles on. When he entered the door, she threw herself onto him and kissed him. For a moment he forgot what he was doing and moved with her in his arms to the sofa, she didn't mind the turned off lights since it was more romantic like this. She unbuttoned his shirt and he tried to calm her a little, but she had missed him so much that she couldn't wait a minute longer. Neither could he.

They kissed passionately and since he had missed her touch so much, he couldn't keep it together. Suddenly he knew he needed to stop her "Celia, wait a minute, I need to tell you something. I love you, I've loved you all these years and being without you is unbearable for me. But I need you to love me, David, not Joe, at least not like this. I can't make love to you knowing that you think I'm someone else." They were both standing in their underwear, with lust in their hearts and for Celia, she couldn't take it anymore. "But it's you. You're my husband, I can't deny you, my body aches for your touch. Does it matter that I can't remember our lives together but still remember every touch?" Joe was the voice, but the touch? "The kisses, it's you, my husband." David moved away from her to the window to think for a moment. She came up from behind him, felt his naked torso underneath her hands and he held her hands towards him. "I know you know me, it's just so painful to see you not knowing me all those weeks. You were so damaged and I couldn't do anything about it, I couldn't even make you remember me." She felt water dripping onto her hands, he was crying, Celia turned David around and kissed him on the lips. He couldn't resist to her kisses and held onto her, unable to let her go. She looked into his eyes, moved her hand to the lamp nearby and turned it on. His eyes, hurt and distressed by the light and his feelings laying bare gave her a view of what had happened approximately a month ago: a man chasing her, her trying to defend herself and then it was all black until now. She moved her hand to his face, followed his nose, passing through his lips and finished on his jawline.

"David?" she said, and he was in shock, she said his name, but did she remember him? For real?

"I know you, we're married. Joe's dead, a long time ago and I think I got into a fight, that's why I couldn't remember us. But I love you, I really do." She said, crying now. The pain she suffered after the first blow, she remembered it all. He helped her sit down for a moment, got a blanket from the cupboard, and put it on her shoulders. "Hey hey, I'm here, I'm here honey and I'm not going anywhere. I told you that same night to wait for me, I was going to pick you up but then I got a call, was delayed and then they called from the hospital telling me you were…badly injured. I was desperate and so mad at myself for not getting to you sooner, it's my fault that you lost your memory." They held each other's hands for a while, Celia was calm and tried to calm him too. She removed the blanket and sat in his lap, his cold arms became warm, and she placed her face underneath his face. David moved to reach her lips, they tasted salty after his tears and she touched his face, it felt like home again. She kissed him, he didn't resist this time and she took his hand to lead him back to their bed. He groaned at her guidance, to feel her undress him the little he was wearing made him aroused and she pushed him carefully onto the bed. Celia climbed on top of him, feeling his erection underneath her, waiting, but right now she was only interested in kissing his torso to make him feel secure. He moved his hands up and down her back, touched her face more than once to bring her closer to his lips.

She giggled a little, which was a good sign for him after these months of just waiting for her to get better. He tried to say something, but she didn't let him, she didn't need apologies, she needed actions. David couldn't wait anymore, he turned her over to have her laying on the bed with still her bra and panties on but removed them slowly. She stretched her arms up as he felt her skin burn up with passion at his touch, it was the only woman that could feel that. The only one he needed. His past, present and future.

CHAPTER 28:
NEW YEARS RESOLUTIONS

Christmas with the family, Celia was recovering almost completely from her injuries but still suffered from nightmares since she could now describe her attacker to the police.

She took some time off from work, decided to do some from home and rely on her secretary to do more. Wrote down on her calendar to give the girl a raise, she had truly been a rock in both good times and bad. Celia had also bought her a nice Christmas present: a gift certificate for a SPA treatment. She surely needed that after many hours of well-done work, a few days off wouldn't be a problem either.

David was feeling better too, his guilt over her accident was slowly fading down, even though he from time to time reminded her that he was the reason she was beat up. Maybe he needed some counseling, she went to a therapist as well, to get rid of her fears of walking close to parks, even in daylight.

New Years was approaching, and Celia was making dinner while David was setting the table, this time they were alone. Ally was in Canada with her boyfriend, soon to be her husband since he had proposed on Christmas which they celebrated in the UK with them. Celia's mom and dad were at home with Claire and her family, surely Celia and David had already been there during the day to have lunch, but the eve was all for them.

"It smells good, want me to do something else? Maybe help you chop some veggies or maybe even, do a little dancing?" he said and gave her a cheeky smile. Celia laughed a little, she threw a piece of carrot to him, and he snagged it in the air "Ahh nice catch, well you could check if the gravy is getting ready and then I need a kiss in advance, otherwise I won't be able to sit still during dinner." She said and smiled to him, he came over, nibbled her neck gently, whispering "Well, we could always eat naked you know, I've got no problem with that." He placed his hand on her waist and moved down a little, grasped her butt cheek a little. "Turn off the food or put it on low, I want you, now." He whispered and walked away, she turned the stove on low heat and went after him.

David was dancing in the bedroom, she stood by the door, smiling. How could a man be so perfect in so many ways, not just his body and not just the sex but his heart. That's what's perfect. She joined in his dancing routine, but instead of going to the bed, they went back to the kitchen "Dessert is for after dinner babe." He teased her.

It was 10:30 pm and they were finishing up their New Years dinner, happy and smiling. David took up his glass of champagne and said "Cheers to you baby, for being the best wife, the best company and the only woman besides my daughter that I will love forever. I love you." Celia was very emotional, she dried a tear from her eye and clinked his glass, now it was her turn "David, I didn't think it could be possible to be happy, healthy, and to have such a great man as you. I love you, always."

He smiled big, clinked her glass, and got up to kiss her. She began putting away the things after dinner and he helped. They would have done food until the next few days, which was good so she wouldn't have to cook anything. He started the dishwasher, turned some slow music on and asked her to dance.

The fireworks started, it had to be around 11 pm, the text messages began coming into her inbox: her parents, sister and husband, friends, family members and Ally. They all sent their best wishes for the upcoming year, she sent back and suddenly it was countdown to midnight.

David held on to her while watching the fireworks from their balcony, he whispered "I want you to know, that I wouldn't have any other way." She turned to kiss him at exactly midnight, the well-known lucky kiss. The kind that you only have with the person you'll live with the rest of your life.

The kiss took them back inside, to the bedroom: he took of her dark blue dress and sat down on the bed to admire her. Her black lace underwear turned him on, even more to see her take it off. She moved towards him, slowly, teasing him. He took her hands when she stretched them to grab his, he sat up closer to the edge of the bed. Celia let go of his hands, moved closer to him to relieve him from his white shirt and black suit pants. As she began unbuttoning his shirt, he placed his hand along her waist, caressing her carefully. He was bare chested now, her favorite way to watch him.

Not because he had a six pack, he was just gorgeous that way: little freckles along his chest, a tiny belly that could barely be seen.

She pushed him onto the bed, he tried to grab a hold of her waist, but she took his hands and pulled them above his head "Don't move" and went to their closet, pulled out one of his ties. He saw the tie in her hands but didn't really understand what she was going to do, she tied his hands lightly and told him to keep them up. Celia unbuttoned his pants, already seeing his erection from underneath them. She smiled to herself and pulled his pants down, then his boxers, releasing him. There he was naked and at her mercy, she smiled again and sat on top of him, since he couldn't touch her, he became even more excited, which she could tell. Celia touched his torso with her fingertips, like she was painting, he flinched because she knew he was ticklish. She moved closer to his chest and pressed herself against him, felt his warmth ooze out almost like opening an oven. He took a deep breath, trying not to move too much even though the tie couldn't possibly hold him for too long. She was still pressed to his chest, blew a little at his erected nipples before she kissed them seductively. He groaned, couldn't keep still and she whispered in his ear "Hold still." David tried to nibble her ear but couldn't reach, she kissed him instead. His breath was warm, like fire in her mouth, and she wanted nothing more than to release his hands so he could hold her in his strong arms and make love to her.

But lately, he had done all the work and made her happy in every possible way and now she just wanted to return the favor. She stopped kissing him and looked in his eyes, he was fired up, ready to go but she didn't want him to move yet. Her mouth moved down, to his chest and nipples, he groaned again. She wasn't fighting fair, he thought but she would get a piece of his mind as soon as this was over, in the best way possible.

She giggled, so did he, called her crazy in a low voice, she released him from his tied hands. He grabbed her waist and pulled her down, kissed her intensively before entering her in full effect. She moaned loud, didn't want him to stop. It was the best sex they ever had, well they've had some nice nights but this, it was a turn on.

They were asleep, he purred to her ear a good morning before grabbing his robe from the floor. He took a good look at his wife, still very much asleep and found the tie on the floor. As a couple they weren't into the "50 shades" style but they way she did it, it was great, something he wanted to try again.

He brushed his teeth and checked the fridge; he would make some pancakes for his love before waking her up. Soon, it would be her birthday and he was thinking about what to get her. She wasn't much for clothes nor shoes, her perfume was always CK's One and jewelry, well she wore her wedding band and had a few other silver rings in her jewelry box but she wasn't that kind of woman.

Celia appreciated quality time, travelling, being with family and her husband, having fun, laughing. She never was a material girl, more like a love life girl. He smiled to himself while he flipped pancakes, surprised that she was still asleep. When he was done, he turned off the heat, put the frying pan in the sink and went to check on her.

CHAPTER 29:
HEAVENLY MEETING

Celia woke up on a green field, amongst flowers and wild grown grass. It was warm but not enough to make her sweat. She didn't know where she was but it felt so normal, that she wasn't even afraid. Walking down on the big field, she saw a road of flowers in different colors and a man standing at the end of it.

She couldn't see who he was but continued, soon she heard someone yell "I knew you would make it here, I've missed you." Celia smiled, but still didn't manage to understand neither where she was nor who the mystery man was. As she came closer, she could see that the man standing there, very much alive was her late husband, Joe. He was wearing a linen shirt and pants, kind of the same as he wore in Hawaii where they had been on vacation and in his hand a purple hortensia, her favorite.

He ran towards her, she stood by and let him hug her. Celia recognized his hug, his voice and finally his kiss "Joe…it's you. That means?" They walked to the closest bench, sat down to talk "Yeah, you are, here time goes very slow but in real time, it's been 2 weeks since you passed, and it takes some time to get here. You know, they just let in the good people, the others well, they go someplace else. I know, your family is devastated for your death, but they will move on, I know it. David, he's very sad because he loves you, more or less than I do but he also knows that you didn't belong to him in the first place. You and I, we belong."

Celia dried her tears, Joe put his arm around her, and she moved away. He didn't understand her negativity but moved to her side again and she ran away to the field. He shouted for her but she didn't stop, of course he was faster and catch up with her by tripping her to the ground. Landing on top of her, he realized she was crying and moved away her face to prevent him from kissing her "Why are you resisting? I still love you like the first moment we met, our date night in New York that ended in your apartment, remember?"

She pushed him away, sat up and he stayed in front of her on his knees. Joe took her hands and pulled them to his chest, it wasn't real to have him in front of her. "I can't, I just, can't." Celia got up and walked away, she felt like her heart was getting ripped from her chest. Maybe she didn't love you anymore or was it because they hadn't seen each other in a long time. She stopped by a tree in full bloom, a fig tree. She remembered something her mom had told her, about this folk tale about the night of S:t John, that women who wanted to know who they were marrying should walk out by midnight to a fig tree and find a flower. At the same time, they needed to avoid the Devil that could take them away. But today wasn't S:t John's night and it was just an afternoon in the sunset, in heaven.

Joe stood by a few meters away, trying to give her space. She was confused with the journey there, he remembered when he first arrived. He didn't know anyone and when he finally could talk to someone, it had been a shock.

He saw Celia crying again, pacing back and forth, he couldn't let her be in such pain "Hey, you, okay?". She had tears in her eyes, couldn't keep it together anymore and she walked to his arms in a rush. Joe held her tight, comforted her before whispering "The sadness you're feeling, it will soon calm down honey. Just give it a chance, I won't pressure you to love me but I'm here for you. Whatever you need."

She listened to his voice, now she realized how tired she was and that a nap would do her good "I'm tired, can we just, go to sleep?". He guided her from the fig tree to this little house on the other side of the field, there were hortensia bushes in different colors and it felt like a home. "This is yours?" she said and admired the painting on the walls, it was so perfect that no flaws could be seen.

He opened the door, let her go in first and it reminded her a little to their home in the Hamptons, when they were married. She sat down in a sofa, close to the window and Joe came back with a blanket from the bedroom: "Here, sleep for a while, I'm going to make us some dinner." Celia curled up in the sofa and fell asleep, Joe stroked her hair and gave her a kiss on the forehead.

She was asleep, dreaming about fields of fruit trees, flowers and Joe, their life before all this. When she woke up, the smell of food made her walk to the kitchen. He was cooking, the table was set and some candles.

Everything smelled fantastic and she was really starving, she stroked his back and said "Hey, what are you cooking?" He smiled, took a spoon and gave her a taste "It's boeuf bourguignon, instead of making it with potatoes,

I made some rice. What do you think?" She closed her eyes and enjoyed the rich taste, well, Joe had always been a great cook, and she missed his food.

"Well ma'am have a seat, I'll be with you shortly. What would you like to drink? We have water, sparkling and still, wine but I know you don't drink oh and iced tea." He said and she sat down, with a smile she told him that iced tea would be great, he poured the tea and served the meal. "Mind if I say Grace? It's a tradition here, you know." "Please, go ahead." She replied and took his hand "I thank you Lord for these gifts we're about to receive. To have my wife here, with me is truly a gift and I can't thank you enough. I've missed her and I hope, in your infinite Grace that she'll love me again. Amen." They let go of their hands but kept looking at each-other, it was like that night in New York, on their date. "Don't worry, I won't push you into anything. I understand that I might be a stranger to you now, but I'm very patient… I'm sure…" Celia interrupted him by giving him a kiss on the lips, he wasn't ready for it but it didn't take any time for him to kiss her back. "I remember" she whispered, and he could feel her breath on his lips, all he wanted was to hold her again, like they used to but he didn't want to scare her off again. She waited for him to grab her waist but realized that he was sitting on his hands to keep himself steady.

"What are you doing?" she said, he smiled and took out his hands from underneath his thighs to show her, but she was so close that he couldn't wait anymore. Joe took her face in his hands, caressed her rosy cheeks with his thumbs before kissing her. His tears wet her face and she sat across his legs to sit better, he smiled to the idea of having her like this again.

"Hey, can we postpone this a little till after dinner? It's not like we don't have time to be happy, and all I want is for you to be happy." He spoke calmly, knowing that a negative could affect her emotional state, but she held him close in a hug and said "Of course, besides, this dinner is worthy of being eaten." She got up from his lap, sat down again and they had their dinner in silence. Joe was uncertain if Celia still loved him as much as she did back then, so he held back, she was helping him with the dishes but didn't say anything. She was quiet, looked happy but looks can sometimes deceive so he asked her, as she put away the plates "Are you okay?". She sighed quietly, looked at him and suddenly they were back in the New York night: Celia threw the cloth on the table and threw herself into his arms, he locked a tight grip of her waist, answering the kiss she had begun. Their breaths interlocked and once again they were one, he unbuttoned her dress underneath smiles, nervous chuckles and kisses. She didn't stay behind, she had already ripped apart his shirt and threw it on the floor. His cold neck was particularly tasty, and he felt how aroused he was becoming, still, the fear of Celia becoming closed again scared him. She noticed and asked, "Do you want to stop?"

He nodded and asked her to sit down next to her in the bedroom, she was calm, out of breath but calm "Look, I don't want to push you into doing something that you don't want to. Maybe now, in the heat of the moment you want to have sex with me but then if you regret it, I couldn't bear something like that."

Celia caressed his face, like she used to when they were married and kissed his cheek. He closed his eyes, feeling her touch was like getting burned but also how much he wanted her and didn't want her to stop "It's not like I don't want to, because I do. Otherwise, I could keep sleeping on the couch until you feel secure, but right now, there's nothing I want more than to be with you. It's true, I loved and still love David, because he picked up the pieces you left. That's how badly it was, you were taken from me. Someone stepped in, someone I have a history with, and it worked out. I didn't forget you, but I moved on to him 100%. Now I'm confused because I'm here with you and I still need you, I still need you to touch me, to make love to me or even if it's just sex. Maybe it will take time for me to adapt but it's not like I have another choice."

"Maybe we should take it slow, work on being a couple again." He said, picked up his shirt, realized it was ripped, went to the wardrobe, and took out a simple white t-shirt.

"How? We are in the same house, that has a sofa and a bed. Why can't we just try again?" she said and readjusted her dress, by the look in her eyes, she wasn't very happy to be rejected like this. She felt ashamed.

"The moment's gone and actually it's better like this, we need time and now, here, all we have is time. We don't grow old here, so even if we wait, we'll be the same.

Please Celia, be patient, okay? Come on, I'll show you to your house."

House? I have my own house. She thought to herself and saw that now there was a house next door. It had her favorite colors, her things in order and the same clothes she used to wear. The fridge and pantry were fully stocked, it would seem like Joe did some grocery shopping before she arrived. But how did it work there? Did she need to do that later, could she shop for clothes or food? Did she have any friends?

He stopped the tour for a minute, he could tell her distress and said "Ask me anything, I'll try to fill you in how it works here. What do you want to know?" Celia sighed; it was a lot of questions "Do I have to shop for food or clothes? Who can I spend time with besides you? Is it always sunny and warm?"

He sat down om the sofa, she did the same with a distance "No, everything restocks after you use it. There's always new clothes in your wardrobe, there's no need to wash anything well unless you're really bored. Here, there are no dust bunnies so there's no vacuums but you can you know wash a glass, a plate if you want. Otherwise, the next morning all will be cleaned and put back in it's place.

I'm the only one here that you know, others live in other areas, but you must make a request to meet them. Usually if you're feeling calm and secure, your request is granted. If not, it says pending."

She got up to the window, with a sense of emptiness and he went to her side "I know it's a lot to take in, I promise to guide you in any way I can. But for now, it's best to start tomorrow. You need to rest and be alone for a while, think what you really want and tomorrow we can talk, okay? Goodnight honey, sleep tight." Joe kissed her head and closed the door behind him.

Celia sighed, went to the closet to find something to sleep in. There was a lot to choose from: regular pajamas, nightgowns, and sexy lingerie. She grabbed one of the thin t-shirts and pants, a towel and went to the bathroom. It was a big bathroom, very neatly decorated, with music but she couldn't see the stereo. The tune was melancholic, it adjusted to her mood and now she felt truly lost.

There wasn't a clock in her house or anywhere, not even in a jewelry box in the bookcase. It was dark out, since she wouldn't have Joe come over again, she might as well go to bed. She hummed "Broken Vow", sat down on the sofa with a blanket over her knees. She must've fallen asleep there because the sun was now rising and shining in her face. She sat up to stretch her arms and saw that she was in bed with covers on, Joe had moved a chair close to her and was asleep.

Celia smiled, he must've carried her to the bed when he found her sleeping in the sofa. He was wearing pajama pants and a t-shirt, his mouth was pursed, like he was trying to kiss someone in his sleep. She watched him for a while, a sense of warmth filled her heart and she couldn't resist anymore.

CHAPTER 30:
FALLING IN LOVE,
ALL OVER AGAIN

Carefully Celia opened her covers to move closer to him, stood so close to feel his breath on her lips. She pressed an innocent kiss on his lips, hoping not to wake him. He woke up and kissed her back, when she intensified the kiss, he couldn't resist.

With their lips still on each other, he got up from the chair and got into bed with her in his arms. She pulled off his t-shirt to feel his warm skin underneath her hands, they smiled shyly towards each other but now he couldn't stop himself; he took off her clothes, kissed her shoulders, her breasts and moved to enter her. Celia moaned to his ear, he smiled with the feeling of having her again after being apart for so long. It was a feeling of needing to be loved and lust, nothing had changed between them.

Joe woke up first, saw her laying on his chest, naked with the bedsheet covering her back. He kissed her head, smelled her hair, stroking her bare back. It was surreal for him to wake up next to her, almost like a beautiful dream. A tear escaped his eye, he chuckled quietly, and she woke up. She looked up to him and smiled, kissed each other good morning "Morning honey, slept well?". Celia moved over, covered up a little and said, "How could I not, last night was interesting."

Joe blushed, that was a new thing. Never during their 5 years had he blushed in her presence, but she was happy to be the cause of it. "Yeah, it was, I know I said we needed time but I couldn't resist you. It wasn't that you were so inviting but more like I had missed you so much and any opportunity to have you back wasn't something I was going to waste. You're the only one, and I love you." The last words were a whisper, but she could feel them. "I love you too."

They hugged and got up to have some breakfast, she admired Joe from the table and felt like everything was a dream. Finally, she was in perfect harmony. She closed her eyes for a while, too much sun in the kitchen. She could still hear Joe making breakfast to her.

"Celia? Celia? Can you hear me?" Mom? Celia thought in her head, she couldn't move but was waking up. She sat up in bed, rubbing her eyes and noticed a bunch of cables in her arms, oxygen mask on her face. Where was she?

"Oh honey, thank God you're okay. The doctor says you'll be alright, the bump on the head wasn't serious and you'll be home in a few days." Her mother was happy, almost teared to see her. Celia still didn't understand, only that this was a hospital, and her head was wrapped in gauze.

She looked at her hands, besides the needle in her hand they looked the same but no wedding band and no husband in the room. "Mom, where's Joe?" she asked, her voice sounded so young, but her mind was still grasping what strange things were happening.

"Honey, who's Joe? Your doctor's name is Steve and he's old enough to be your father." Her mother looked concerned, maybe the bump in her head was more serious than she imagined.

"Mom, what date is today?" she said, still confused, but even more when her mother responded "July 15th, 1994, you were at camp and your stepfather insisted on you going sailing, even though the storm was coming in. The boat's mast hit you in the head and you've been in the hospital for 2 weeks in a coma. You don't remember?"

July 1994, would mean she was 12 years old and everything she lived was just a dream?

"Mom, I was married, you were there with Claire. It wasn't, real?" she said, tears overflowed her eyes. Everything she felt, everything she went through was just that. Joe and David were figments of her imagination. The doctor came through the door to check up on her, he ordered a CT to see what was going on in her brain but Celia didn't want anything.

"Can I please be alone? I need, to rest." She said and the doctor asked the nurse to give her a sedative, clearly the patient needed something for her anxiety. Everyone left and closed the door.

Celia went to the bathroom and looked at herself in the mirror, there she was, 12 years old again with nothing else but the sensation of feeling what being in love with a man felt like. She washed her face and went back to bed; the sedative was flowing in her bloodstream and once again she was falling into deep sleep.

August 9, 2020

Celia was coming out of the doctor's office, she had just got a job as a receptionist in a small clinic in Birmingham, UK. She was happy, at last she could work in a place that she liked with a great pay. She called her mother but she didn't respond, she called her sister and she said "I'm in class, can I call you back?"

Celia said "Yeah, call me on your break. It's important." They hung up, so Celia walked towards the metro station to get back home. A guy was standing in front of her in the queue at Prêt a Manger, funny how he had the same noodle salad as she. The mere thought made her smile but forgot to put it away, so he thought she was smiling to him.

"Hi." He said and she looked surprised, normally guys didn't hit on her very often or more specific, never because she wasn't a catch as some said. She wasn't very tall, didn't have long legs and was not model like. Celia was just her: round with round face, 1,63 meters with a sense of style that didn't really appeal to guys. But she found it comfortable, that's what she aimed for: comfort.

"Hi." She replied and continued to pay, the guy waited for her until she was finished and packing her noodle pack. He stood up, approached her on the way out and said "Sorry, I normally don't do this but I just find you so pretty. I felt the need to ask for your name and if you want to have some coffee with me."

Celia looked even more confused; the guy was almost 1,80 meters tall, short dark hair, black glasses, brown eyes, dressed in a sweater and jeans with a backpack. He was cute, but why did he find her attractive in her jeans and t-shirt? There were other girls in the convenience store in high heels and dresses.

"Uh, sure, but no coffee for me. Tea perhaps?" she replied, didn't really know why she said that but thought what the hell right? He wouldn't be the first to ask her out and then tell her that she wasn't the right one.

They walked together to the nearest Starbucks, he opened the door for her and stood by the counter to order "What would you like to drink? My treat." He said and looked shyly at her, she smiled back and said "A hot chocolate please, no marshmallows nor cream. You?" "The same, oh and want to split a muffin?" She chuckled; he knew she liked sweet things.

They got their order and went to the table by the window, he let her sit first and sat down in front of her. She drank a little from her cup and waited for him to say something, he smiled and seemed somehow familiar to her. Maybe they had eye contact before during visits to Prêt a Manger or some other place nearby "Can I have your name?" he said, almost whispering.

His voice made the hairs on her arms raise underneath her jacket. Why did he have that effect on her? A random guy, handsome yes but guys like that didn't fall for girls like her. She could be a best friend but never someone's love interest, her younger years were pretty much a disaster when it came to love. Maybe that's why she stayed away.

Her mother had told her once before that she should never give out her name but really, how many were named like her in the city? She gave him a weak smile, her legs tingling at the sight of his beautiful eyes perfectly framed in his glasses "My name is Celia, you?"

"Nice to meet you Celia, I'm Joseph but you can call me Joe…"

PLAYLIST FOR "WINDOWS TO THE SOUL"

HIM "WICKED GAME" (DATING DAVID)

ROBIN THICKE "BLURRED LINES" (DATING DAVID)

ELTON JOHN "CAN YOU FEEL THE LOVE TONIGHT"
(HAWAII)

GEORGE MICHAEL "CARELESS WHISPER"
(HAWAII LATE NIGHT)

JAMES BLUNT "THE ONLY ONE" (FIRST DATENIGHT IN
NEW YORK)

JAMES BLUNT "BONFIRE HEART" (JOE'S PROPOSAL)

SARAH BRIGHTMAN "AVE MARIA" (WEDDING)

LUIS FONSI FEAT DADDY YANKEE "DESPACITO" (NIGHT
OF LOVE)

ROBBIE WILLIAMS "ANGELS" (JOE'S FUNERAL)

GEORGE MICHAEL "DON'T LET THE SUN GO DOWN"
(FIRST NIGHT ALONE AGAIN)

TAKE THAT "BACK FOR GOOD" (LEAVING NEW YORK)

GEORGE MICHAEL "PRAYING FOR TIME"
(TOGETHER AGAIN WITH DAVID)

CELINE DION "BECAUSE YOU LOVED ME" (DAVID)

SIA "CHEAP THRILLS" (CELIA)

BOYZONE "COMING HOME NOW" (JOE)

ANDREA BOCELLI "CON TE PARTIRO" (WAKING UP)

LUCIFER CAST FEAT. TOM ELLIS "CREEP" (MEETING
AGAIN)

IMAGINE DRAGONS "BELIEVER" (ENDING)